RHITT DAVIS, COUNTRY CLUB CHAMPION GOLFER, HAS A LIFE THAT MOST PEOPLE ONLY DREAM OF, ENTERTAINING THE CLIENTS OF ONE OF LOS ANGELES' PRESTIGIOUS PUBLIC RELATIONS FIRMS.

BUT . . ..

The disappearance of a close friend draws him into a sinister string of events that involve a convicted gambler, a beautiful FBI informant, and someone determined to serve Hollywood's A-List a lethal dose of revenge.

ANGELS GATE

A Rhitt Davis Thriller

—

By

John Scheibe

ENCINO
MEDIA

Copyright ©2018 by John Scheibe
Edited by Elena Howe
Cover Illustration ©2018 by Kathy Varie
Book Designed by Siri Weber Feeney

ENCINO MEDIA
818-317-9349
jps126@earthlink.net

ISBN-13: 978-0-9793709-1-5
ISBN-10: 0-9793709-1-4
Printed in the United States of America

—

To my Mom, Donna,
who was an inspiration
to writers young and old
when she worked in
Hollywood
and later,
in the newspaper
business.

—

PROLOGUE

The water inside the rock jetty was so smooth it looked like dark-blue glass in the moonlight. It reflected the lights from the nearby waterfront, with its fishing boats that had spent the day at sea and restaurants opened for their early evening customers, glittered across its surface.

As the last of the sunlight had faded below the horizon, the 20-foot sail boat *Singular* quietly maneuvered past the breakwater rocks, and sailed under the twin light spires of Angels Gate into the main channel of Los Angeles Harbor.

The *Singular* had put to sea five days earlier from a small yacht marina along the central coast of California near San Simeon, and had made an overnight stop on the second day in Santa Barbara. There it took aboard four large wooden crates, the sealed contents of which were carefully wrapped in newspaper and straw packing, then nailed shut and sealed with duct tape.

The boat, which had a crew of two men

dressed in jeans, heavy jackets and knit caps, observed the five mile-per-hour speed limit as it made its way past the harbor's fire boat house and under the Vincent Thomas bridge, the long span that connected San Pedro with the port of Long Beach to the southeast. The *Singular* followed the channel as it made a right turn toward the smaller Ford drawbridge. A crewman cut the auxiliary motor and guided the boat to a slip where another man in dark clothing and wearing a baseball cap, was waiting on the dock. He clicked his flashlight twice at the approaching boat, which eased quietly into the slip.

The man secured the yacht's bow, fore and aft, with two nylon ropes and helped the crewmen unload the four crates onto the landing. All three wore heavy rubber gloves, the kind plumbers wear when cleaning out a main water line or sewer drain.

The four crates were stacked on a dolly and rolled to the end of the landing where a late-model Mercedes-Benz was parked. A woman with shoulder-length brown hair dressed in dark slacks, a suede jacket and aviator sunglasses opened the trunk of the big German import as they approached.

"Make sure they are flat," the woman

instructed as they loaded in the crates.

While they adjusted the cargo, she took a large roll of cash from her purse and paid each man $2,500. Then, without a word, she closed the trunk, got in the car and drove down the partially paved road that connected the dock with Pacific Coast Highway, and then soon blended in with the night's flow of traffic.

Chapter One
THE MAGNOLIA HOLE

It was one of those late fall days in Los Angeles where the temperature could drop 35 degrees from noon to sunset around six o'clock. Rhitt Davis decided to take a sweater because it would be chilly by the time he and Maurice Otto reached the 10th tee at the Wilshire Club.

Davis was playing golf with Otto, one of Karl Stoddard and Associates' wealthier clients. Otto was a king in the kosher food business, with labels of meats, fish and traditional Jewish holiday fare, all sold at finer markets in L.A., New York and in central and south Florida. Also, as a former president of one of Hollywood's older studios, Enterprise Pictures, he kept his hand in the business by occasionally co-producing a low-budget movie.

His influence in the cinema world, however, had been greatly reduced by a string of misfires at the box office. His authority in green-lighting a movie had also been diminished with the arrival of a new generation of studio heads and filmmakers. At times, especially after a few drinks, his resentment at being pushed aside by the younger Hollywood crowd would emerge like the biting chill of a cold wind.

"I got side-swiped by a bunch of punks, most of whom never read a script or knew one end of a camera from the other. Their big talent was kissing the right ass."

Now, Otto spent most of his time at Wilshire, sitting out the morning on the clubhouse veranda, reading the newspaper or playing cards with other club members, and at least one afternoon a week he tried to beat Davis in golf, which was nearly impossible because Davis was an under-par player and, on a good day, Otto could barely break into the high 80s.

Still, Davis was under strict orders from the agency's president Karl Stoddard to "whip Otto's ass."

"I want you to bury him," Stoddard shouted one night after Otto had come within two strokes of winning a round. Davis had gotten bored on the back nine and decided to experiment with his swing and grip, trying among other things to put spin on the ball with a hard six-iron instead of hitting a normal five on a 185-yard approach. Earlier, the experimenting had led to his ball landing in bunkers, and sent one tee shot out-of-bounds, and Otto, who was playing better than usual, took advantage by making three birdies.

"I don't want him bragging to his cronies at the bar that he almost beat you," fumed Stoddard. His strategy of offering rounds of golf to current and prospective clients such as Otto at a prestigious club such as the Wilshire with the opportunity to play Davis, a former western U.S. amateur champion, was nearly irresistible.

Davis put his clubs in the bed of his pickup truck and drove south from his second-floor flat at Franklin and La Brea avenues in Hollywood to Beverly Drive and then east on Beverly to Larchmont Avenue where he turned into the parking lot at the Wilshire Club. He parked in Stoddard's slot and Eddie Stiles, one of the club's parking attendants, took his clubs, sweater and shoes.

"Beautiful afternoon to play, Mr. Davis," Stiles said as he greeted him. "Do you want to go to the locker room first?"

Davis gestured toward the tee box, which was just in sight of the clubhouse.

"Mr. Otto again?" asked Stiles. Davis let out a small sigh and said, "Yes, Otto, again."

Stiles nodded and Davis followed him through to the nearly empty men's locker room and out to where Otto was waiting in a cart with their caddy, Freddy Lopez, an older Latino man who at one time carried Bing Crosby's bag when the crooner would stop by for nine holes before going to work at nearby Paramount Studios.

"I had breakfast with your boss this morning, Mr. Davis, and he gave me a tip on how to gain a few strokes on you," Otto said as he lit a cigar. Davis looked at Lopez who carefully folded Davis' sweater and then placed it neatly in the basket in the back of Otto's cart. A faint smile crossed Lopez's face.

"Mr. Stoddard knows how to create distractions. What is it, something original like sneezing in my backswing? Just between you and me, I don't think Karl has picked up a golf club in years."

"No, no, nothing that would step over the line of etiquette," Otto puffed. "Something more attractive, such as offering you an executive position in Enterprise's public relations department."

Lopez's smile turned to a wide grin, his white teeth shimmering against his lined tanned skin.

"Now, that is a tempting distraction," Davis said, as he slipped on his black, Kangaroo-skin golf shoes. He tied the laces in a neat bow and smoothed his white polo shirt around the waistband of his Navy blue slacks. "But I sold my soul to the devil when I signed on with Karl Stoddard & Associates."

Lopez choked back a laugh and put Davis' bag over his shoulder. Otto teed up his ball and hit a nice drive down the center of the fairway. Otto gave his driver to Lopez and said, "Well, seeing as how you are so gainfully employed, Mr. Davis, how about increasing our wager to $50 a hole, double on the par 3s and $100 for birdies?"

Davis took his 3-iron from the bag and dropped his ball between the blue tee markers. He aimed for the right side of the fairway and, with no warmup, took his swing, shaping a perfect right-to-left draw that caught the mild breeze and flew past Otto's ball by 50 yards.

"Sure, Maurice." Davis said, "as long as there's something in it for Freddy."

Davis gave the caddie his club and waited behind as Lopez and Otto rode up the fairway to Otto's ball. He took a pack of cigarettes out of his pocket and lit one with a sterling silver lighter that Stoddard had given him when he joined the public relations firm. Engraved on the front was the line "Never on Sunday," Stoddard's way of reminding him about certain vices, including smoking cigarettes.

Davis began smoking when he was in college, but quit when he decided to make a run at becoming a professional golfer. Back-to-back West Coast Amateur titles and a year of playing on a minor pro tour in the Southeast gave him the momentum to try to qualify for a PGA tour card. At the qualifying school tournament, he stayed with the leaders for three rounds, but fell back and was eliminated when the weak part of his game, his putting stroke, disappeared on the back nine of the final round. He missed qualifying by one shot. He gave it another try the following year but the result was the same.

He took a drag on the Winston and as he exhaled he gazed at the vista before him, the hills, as clear and close as if he could reach out and touch the Hollywood sign or tap the domes of the Griffith Park Observatory with the grip of his 3-iron. It certainly was a sight he would seldom have gotten to see if he had agreed to work on the night copy desk at the Daily News' sports department.

Suddenly he heard Freddy Lopez call out, "Mr. Davis, you're away." He turned and jogged up the fairway to his ball.

Davis and Otto both had par on the first hole and after they teed off on the second, Lopez walked alongside Davis.

"How come you got yourself into a shark business like public relations, Mr. Davis? I would think working for a sports department of a big city newspaper, goin' to all the games and seein' and writin' about the big leaguers would be a lot more fun than having to play golf with guys like Mr. Rhythm and Blues over there." He gestured toward Otto.

Davis looked at Otto then jammed his hands into his pockets.

"I was forced out. I was dating a woman who was good friends with a gambler and he was suspected of having ties to some bad guys, you know, other gamblers.

"The sports editor who hired me to write about golf didn't like it and told me to stop seeing her. I said no and he took me off the beat and put me on the night copy desk. So, I quit."

"That's a flimsy reason, if you ask me," the caddy said. "Aren't sports and gambling kinda like bacon and eggs, they kinda go together?"

Davis explained that the gambler, whose name was Jake Dumont, was no ordinary bookie. Dumont's ties to a crime syndicate were well documented. He had been convicted for shaving points in college basketball games, involving mostly teams from schools on the East Coast. When he got out of prison, he moved to Los Angeles and worked his way into becoming a collector of rare art objects, which included jewelry, sculptures and paintings.

"It didn't matter. I was making more money in a day winning skins at member-guest tournaments than I ever made in two weeks at the paper. That's how I met Karl Stoddard. Maybe the sports editor did me a favor."

Davis stopped at his ball, which was in the center of the fairway, about 112 yards from the front of the green. The flagstick was also in the front. Lopez gave him a sand wedge and Davis lobbed it over the hole. The ball spun back and rolled to within foot of the hole for a tap-in birdie.

Otto applauded from his seat in the cart. "OK, showoff, that'll do."

Otto conceded the hole, picked up his ball and drove to the No. 3 hole, which was called the Magnolia Hole, named for the three large Magnolia trees that guarded the right side of the fairway.

Davis had the honors. The Magnolia Hole was a short par-3, about 125 yards to the center of the green. The trick was to carry the shot over a small ravine that stretched across the front edge of the green. Just as Davis lined up his shot, he heard his cell phone ring. It was inside the pocket of his golf bag.

"You want me to get it?" asked Otto. Davis swore at himself for leaving it on. He knew it was Stoddard. "No...thank you," Davis said. He pulled the phone out and put it to his ear. He heard Stoddard's voice.

"What, you can't afford gas for the Porsche," he said knowing full well Davis preferred the heft of his truck and would have left that in Stoddard's slot.

Davis gestured for Otto to tee off and then walked away so that the old man couldn't hear him.

"I'm on the third hole," Davis said into the phone.

"Give Otto a rematch and tell him you'll buy him lunch as soon as you have an opening in your schedule. Then, come over to Sagebrush."

"Can't it wait?" asked Davis. He heard Stoddard let out a long sigh.

"No, it can't."

Davis pulled a solid gold money clip from his pocket and tipped Freddy Lopez for 18 holes and offered Otto an apology. Then he put on his sweater and, with his clubs slung over his shoulder, walked back up the first fairway to the clubhouse.

Chapter 2
SAGEBRUSH

The building that housed the offices of Karl Stoddard and Associates was located on a tree-lined street a block south of Wilshire Boulevard near the Beverly Wilshire Hotel. It was called Sagebrush by the architect, but it looked more like an Ivy League college dormitory than a Beverly Hills office building, and it suited Stoddard fine because several of his clients' offices were within walking distance, and he could also hold court at lunch at the Palms restaurant at the Beverly Wilshire.

Stoddard had built his business from a studio publicity pool ward, whose work included everything from writing press releases for movie marketing campaigns and re-writing television situation comedies and westerns scripts, to the top crisis management firm on the Westside of Los Angeles.

A list of wealthy and influential clients included religious leaders, professional sports team owners, newspaper and motion picture

executives and heads of successful small busi-
nesses. But it was trouble at one of his sister's art
and health boutiques that prompted him to interrupt Rhitt Davis' golf game with Maurice Otto at
the Wilshire Club.

As Davis drove west toward Beverly Hills,
his conversation with Freddy Lopez made him
recall the last time he saw Patty Baker, a very
close friend who he had first met in college. She
had dated Jake Dumont for over two years and
had briefly lived in a house he owned in the Hollywood Hills. When she moved out, she rented
an apartment on the border of the Los Feliz and
Silver Lake neighborhoods.

One early morning she had telephoned Davis,
waking him out of a fitful sleep, frightened, saying
there were two men outside her door. They had
parked their car at the curb and were taking turns
walking up the brick path to the front, sometimes
peering through her window near the porch.

Davis got dressed and drove east to Vermont
Avenue, then north to her street which was a block
from Los Feliz Boulevard. When he approached
Baker's apartment, he didn't see anyone. He let
himself in with a key that she had given him. In the
dark, he saw her standing in a doorway, dressed
only in a cotton short-sleeved shirt, unbuttoned,

and holding a pistol in her right hand. The porch light highlighted her shoulder-length brown hair and her deeply-tanned arms and legs.

He went to the kitchen and fixed her a light bourbon and water with ice. Then he gently took the gun and put the drink in her hand. She said the two men could have been the police, on a stakeout to gather information on Dumont. She added that she thought her apartment phone had been tapped because she heard clicking and static in the earpiece.

Patty took a sip of the bourbon, and walked to her bedroom. As she was about to close the door she turned to Davis and said, "Or it could have been friends of Jake's. Thanks for coming over, Rhitt."

Davis took off his shoes and lay down on the sofa. He slept there until it got light. When he woke up, Baker was gone. He fixed himself a breakfast of coffee, toast and eggs, and when he was finished, he put the key on the kitchen counter and left.

Now it was a month later and he hadn't seen or heard from her since that morning. Stoddard's building had underground parking, but Davis made a U-turn and parked the Ford F-150 pickup on the street in the closest spot to the Sagebrush.

He smiled because he knew it would annoy his boss if he saw it there.

He went in the front entrance and took the stairs to the second floor of suites. It was warm inside and as he reached the top of the stairs he took off his sweater and gave it to Joyce Myers, one of Stoddard's secretaries. "Go on in," she said, "unless you want to wash up first." Davis shook his head and thanked her.

He walked into Stoddard's office and closed the door. Karl Stoddard was talking on the telephone and when he saw Davis, he ended his conversation and hung up.

"Sorry to break up your afternoon with Otto but he's good for a rematch," said Stoddard, as he walked across the plush carpeted office to gaze out a large Bay window.

"What do you know about health boutiques, holistic remedies, aroma therapies and the like?" Stoddard asked as he turned back to Davis, who had sat down in a chair near Stoddard's desk.

"Not much, but one hears about those kind of health treatments more and more," Davis replied.

"Like the rest of us," Stoddard said. "My sister, Anna, has had some trouble lately with her business over in Los Feliz. She runs a health food store and art gallery up there and twice in the last two months somebody has broken in and messed up the place."

Davis was silent for a few seconds. "What do the police say?"

Stoddard waived his hand in the air, walked back to his desk and sat down.

"Hell, the cops have been little help. Their report called it breaking in and entering because nothing was stolen, just things thrown around the store. She changed the locks but it happened again a few nights ago."

Joyce Myers opened the door. "Sorry to interrupt, Mr. Stoddard," Ben Boyd at ABC is on Line Four."

"I'll be right with him," Stoddard said. He turned back to Davis. "I want you to get a little publicity campaign going for Anna, get some stories in the neighborhood paper, maybe even in *The Times* and *Daily News*, you know, stuff that will pump up her business. It's fallen off considerably since the second break-in. Prettyman will help you."

Davis raised his eyebrows at Stoddard's last remark. "I'd rather do it myself," Davis said.

Stoddard shook his head. "Prettyman knows a lot about the holistic health industry. She'll give you the ideas and you write up the press releases.

Besides, it's time you did something else besides eat lunch and play golf," and Stoddard paused, then said, "it's time for you to expand in this business.

"What about my schedule? I've got rounds at Wilshire with the Fox TV execs."

"Play them then get on this project," said Stoddard. "Let me know how it's going at the end of the week."

Davis stood up, "OK, whatever you want, Karl."

As he walked to the door, Stoddard shouted, "And park that damn truck somewhere where I can't see it."

Davis closed the door and walked past Joyce Myers' desk. "Don't forget your sweater," she said, handing it to him. She had neatly folded it, similar to the way Freddy Lopez had done.

"What do you know about art and health foods, Joyce?"

"I hate to admit it but I don't know one artist from another," she said. "I am into the art of food, and not healthy food. For me, being healthy is not my kind of fun. I drink water out of the tap, and love a martini and a steak, especially if there is a chocolate sundae for dessert."

Davis smiled at her and said, "Now you're talkin'."

———

Rhitt Davis gunned the pickup and headed back to Hollywood. "Prettyman," he thought. Karl Stoddard had hired her to work with the movie studio execs and be on-call to assist with crisis management involving the firm's big clients.

Mary Prettyman was smart and attractive, and very ambitious. She had majored in English and communications at University of California, Berkeley, got her career start in public relations with an internship at one of San Francisco's most successful firms, which later hired her full-time. She quickly established a network of media contacts that included most of the Bay Area's biggest television, radio and newspaper personalities. She had a golden touch for landing star clients.

One was a large hospital in upscale Marin County, one of the few in the Bay Area that offered homeopathic treatment for minor ailments. It was at the Marin hospital that, by coincidence she met Stoddard, who was being treated for a pinched nerve in his neck by an acupuncture therapist. He invited her to have dinner with him and at the appropriate moment offered her a job.

Without much selling from Stoddard, she

accepted, saying she had yearned to work in Los Angeles, and needed a change of climate. She had been engaged to a professional basketball player whose 10-year career was just about over. He wanted her to be a stay-at-home mother while he traveled as a network broadcaster during the pro season. She thought about his wish for all of five minutes, and said, "No, thanks," ending the engagement.

She also said the weather in San Francisco was too chilly most of the year, paraphrasing the famous line by Marilyn Monroe "like an air conditioner that you could never turn off."

Davis had first met her at Sagebrush, with an introduction by Stoddard. He remembered as he said, "It's a pleasure to meet you," that her eyes looked into his for a split second, then shot past him.

But it was at the firm's annual party for its clients at 20th Century Fox's backlot that Davis remembered her making a lasting impression.

Stoddard had put her in charge of overseeing the evening's production, which included guests invited from the industries of entertainment, philanthropy, banking, legal and sports.

She warmly welcomed those who arrived at the main dining area, a large, open-air canopy tent set up on the studio's famed New York City street set.

She looked exquisite in a flowing cream-colored silk blouse and dark slacks that were fitted at the waist and belled out just above her Monola Blahnik heels.

She wore a black onyx Art Deco bracelet on her right wrist and on her left, a gold Patek Phillipe watch.

Her short, Auburn-colored hair was slicked back, like she had just stepped out of a cool shower. Diamond drop earrings shimmered from each earlobe and the light in her liquid hazel eyes was radiant.

Karl Stoddard stood nearby, greeting guests as well, and complimenting her on the job she had done. He repeated over and over, "Wonderful, my dear. Excellent turnout."

Later, Stoddard made sure that she mingled with the right sort and steered her away from the firm's single-male contingent, all of whom stood on the fringe of the show. If she was going to schmooze with anyone it was going to be with the president of the Annenberg Foundation, not a second-tiered flak.

Davis watched from the bar with mild amusement. As he sipped his gin and tonic, he saw the look of frustration and longing on the faces of the men at the firm who had made a play for her, two or three of whom she had brushed off after they worked up the nerve to ask her for a date. They resented her and made raunchy remarks in the locker room at the racquet club.

"Forget it with 'Pretty-tits,'" and other comments that suggested she had broken her engagement not because she didn't want to marry an aging basketball player, but because she was all along involved with one of his former girlfriends.

Davis considered himself lucky that Stoddard hadn't made him, up till now, work with the other members of the staff.

As he drove up La Brea Avenue, his thoughts again turned to Patty Baker, his old flame, who had now disappeared. He had tried phoning her for over a week to see what became of the two men outside her apartment, but she did not return his calls. He even drove past the apartment on Rowena Avenue, but from the front it seemed empty. He didn't know if she had moved back in with Jake Dumont, had left L.A., or if something else had happened to her. Now, suddenly, Stoddard had ordered him to help Mary Prettyman with what seemed to be a silly assignment at his sister's art gallery.

He sensed that Prettyman thought that he was lazy, just a guy who hung out with rich men on a country club golf course and spent the rest of the day at lunch, playing poker in the card room or taking a steam bath in the club's sauna. The assignment could be Karl Stoddard's way of getting back at him for parking his pickup truck in Stoddard's slot at the Wilshire Club. But Karl Stoddard didn't know Patty Baker and he didn't know Jake Dumont and he didn't know what was packed aboard the sailboat *Singular* as it passed through Angels Gate and into L.A. Harbor that quiet night two weeks earlier.

Chapter 3
A FRAGRANT EVENING

Rhitt Davis locked his truck, put his golf bag over his shoulder and walked to his apartment. The building was a Spanish style two-floor villa, with large living quarters on each level. It was nicely spaced between two modern buildings on Franklin Avenue, just west of La Brea in the foothills of Hollywood.

He entered the lobby and walked a few steps to a door that led to a stairway. He opened it with a key and climbed the staircase two steps at a time. He could feel a cool breeze from the hills stir through a balcony terrace that led to his living room.

He opened drapes that covered three large picture windows and suddenly the expansive room was bathed in the glow of the fall afternoon.

A high-beamed ceiling and refinished hardwood floors jumped to life in the sunlight. Davis propped his golf bag against a thick, white plaster wall near the south-facing window. He gazed at the city at his feet, a magnificent vista of Hollywood and beyond.

Patty Baker playfully called it the "three-way room." It had views of the hills to the east, downtown L.A. to the south and, on a clear day, the ocean to the west. The kitchen looked out over Hollywood and the morning sunrise was a magnificent sight.

Patty had found the apartment for him, and considered it a gift for his loyalty when he wouldn't give in to the demand of his conservative newspaper boss to leave her because she had had an affair with Jake Dumont. She wanted to have it decorated for him, but now her disappearance had made that chance, for the moment, unlikely. The only pieces of furniture in the room were a futon sofa and a standing floor lamp with a large white shade.

Davis walked down a hallway to his bedroom where he took off his clothes, throwing his trousers and polo shirt on the bed. The suite had a walk-in closet and a full bathroom. He turned on the water in the shower, grabbed a towel off the rack and rinsed himself off.

Wrapping the towel around his waist, he went to the phone on the nightstand and called one of his favorite restaurants, the Gardens of

Tasco in West Hollywood. He wanted to know what time Angel Campos would be starting work that night. The hostess said Angel would be in a little after 5 o'clock.

Davis thanked her and dressed himself in khaki slacks, a long-sleeved pressed blue dress shirt, dark socks and brown Moccasin shoes. He took a Navy blue blazer that had just been cleaned off the rack, filled his pockets with keys, wallet, cell-phone and a white linen handkerchief, and went downstairs to his garage.

He opened the door and went to the driver's side of a vintage black 911-S Porsche coupe. He hadn't driven it in awhile so it needed a run. He backed it out to the street, closed the garage door with a remote, gave the 2.0 litre engine two or three revs, then slowly made his way down the hill in first gear. Once he reached La Brea he drove quickly to Santa Monica Boulevard, and turned right, heading west.

Angel Campos was the restaurant's assistant manager. Davis had known him for nearly 10 years, since Angel was an exercise rider at Santa Anita and Del Mar race tracks. He began riding as a teenager on quarter horse mounts in Mexico City, then traveled north to Caliente on the California border, and then on to L.A. with a dream of becoming a winning, and money-making jockey.

But his struggle to keep his weight under control wouldn't let him. No matter how hard he exercised and watched his diet, he couldn't lose the pounds. Fortunately, the trainers gave him steady work with the morning workouts and later he found his way into the restaurant business.

Davis let the valet park his car and walked into the Gardens of Tasco. There were a few patrons at the bar, but the main dining room was all but empty. He ordered a beer and asked a waitress to tell Campos that he would meet him at a small booth at the far end of the room.

Davis took off his blazer and sat down. The dining room was cool and dimly lit, highlighted by dark green painted walls and carpeting. He closed his eyes and thought it would be nice to fall asleep for a few minutes. He rested his head against the soft leather of the booth, took a deep breath and was about to stretch his legs out under the table when he heard a voice say, "Senor Rhitt."

Angel Campos stood across from him. Davis immediately sat up.

"It is good to see you again after such a long time, since the tournament in Palm Springs, eh?" Campos said as he extended his hand. The two shook hands and Davis gestured for the former jockey to sit down.

"You are no longer in the sports writing business, I hear," Campos said. "I can tell because you are dressing much more fashionably.

"So, what brings you here, besides the good food and the drink?"

"How good are your gambling connections these days, Angel?"

Campos was silent for a moment, studying Davis' face as he pondered the question.

He smiled and gestured with his hand. "I keep in touch with the old crowd."

Davis laughed, and said, "Does that include Jake Dumont?"

Angel lightly bit his lower lip and smiled thinly. "He is a peculiar man. I saw him a couple times at Del Mar this summer, in the Turf Club. He was betting heavily, like he was trying to lose all his money in one day. Only, he didn't run out of money."

"Have you seen him since?"

"No. He used to come in here, once a month or so, late at night, usually with a woman.

Angel looked at Davis. "Your friend, right?"

"Patricia Baker."

"A beautiful woman. Her elegant, dark features are like the still of the night, very mysterious.

I would prefer that she was with you instead of him."

Davis took a sip from his beer.

"If you see either one of them, Angel, would you give me a call?" Davis took a small notepad and pen from his inside jacket pocket and wrote down his phone number. He tore the paper off the rings and handed it to Campos.

"Anything for you, my friend," Angel said.

At that moment a group of diners sat down in the next booth. He glanced their way.

"I've got to go back to work, Senor. If I find out anything . . . ."

The two men shook hands.

"Angel, here's to fast horses and big winners."

———

When he opened the door back at his flat, he sensed that someone was inside. He turned on the living room lamp and noticed that his golf bag had been moved about a foot from where he originally had propped it against the wall.

He walked to the kitchen, then to the guest bedroom, the master bedroom suite and the balcony, turning on the lights as he went. In the kitchen there was a hint of a fragrance, but he couldn't tell if it was the distant scent of night blooming jasmine, which grew wild in the hills, or something else.

The aroma drifted down the hallway from his bedroom. Davis turned on the light and followed the scent into the bathroom. It was strongest there, and he recognized it as the perfume he had once given Patty, Mademoiselle by Chanel, a fragrance that was spicy and romantic. There were drops of it on the tile counter.

Patty liked the fragrance so much that she would splash it into her bath water. Sometimes when he was asleep, she would put some on her finger and rub it behind his ear or on his neck. The smell from his skin would drive her to blissfully bite his earlobe.

Suddenly, his home phone rang and he hurried into the bedroom to pick up the extension.

A woman's voice said, "Mr. Davis?"

"Yes, this is Rhitt Davis."

"This is Mary Prettyman, from the agency. I was wondering if you might have a little time tonight to discuss our project on Anna Stoddard. I wrote up an outline with a couple ideas and I thought we'd get a head start before our meeting tomorrow."

Davis was caught off guard.

"I wasn't aware of a meeting tomorrow," he said.

"Yes, Mr. Stoddard arranged a get-together in the morning at his sister's gallery. I'm actually not far from your apartment, you're in Hollywood, right?"

"Uh, yes, on Franklin Avenue, 5-0-1-0, a block west of La Brea."

"I'm just coming from a cocktail party at Spago and I rousted up a couple doggie bags of bar food from the party, if you're hungry and it's not inconvenient . . .?"

Davis sat on his bed and ran his hand through his curly black hair. He thought to himself, "That damn Stoddard." Then he said, "No, I'm not busy, I'll leave a parking space for you on the street."

He hung up the phone, went downstairs and moved the pickup truck into the driveway.

Mary Prettyman arrived a few minutes later. She entered his apartment wearing a white Yves St. Laurent wool suit. She held her purse in her right hand and her briefcase was under her right arm. It was balanced by a Louis Vuitton/ Edun leather bag that she had slung over her left shoulder.

She put down the purse and briefcase on the hardwood and extended her hand to Davis. "I'm not sure we've ever officially met," she said.

Davis shook her hand. "I think Karl

introduced us when you came aboard at Sagebrush."

Mary Prettyman smiled. "You have a good memory."

"I've got some treats in my bag here, if you want to eat while we go over the outline."

As Davis showed her the way to the kitchen, she glanced toward the golf clubs, then at the expansive, furnitureless living room.

"Beautiful room, and views, but you could use an interior decorator."

"I've lived here only four months and a friend was going to have that done for me," Davis answered. "But lately she's, uh, she's been out of touch."

Prettyman put her shoulder bag on the kitchen table, unzipped it and removed two brown paper bags with two containers in each one. "It's a mix of Maryland Blue Crab Cannelloni and roasted Sonoma lamb, plus Calzone pizza with artichokes, and I think a little salmon and caviar."

"Sounds almost too delicious to eat," Davis said, "but I'll try the pizza."

Davis got two large plates, serving spoons, napkins and knives and forks. As Mary Prettyman put a combination from each container onto the plates, Davis retrieved two glasses from the dishwasher.

"I've got some wine and/or beer if you'd like?"

"Better make it water. I had some champagne at the party, and I've got to get up early."

She took off her jacket and hung it over the back of one of the kitchen chairs. She unfastened the gold cufflinks from the French cuffs of her long-sleeved blue silk blouse and rolled the sleeves halfway to her elbow. As she was about to sit down she looked back toward the living room and tilted her nose in the air.

"That's a lovely fragrance, Chanel, maybe?"

Davis blushed. "Uh, I spilled some cologne in the bathroom earlier and it's, well, all over the apartment." He gestured with his hand toward the other rooms.

Mary Prettyman laughed. "Are you sure I'm not interrupting anything?"

Davis assured her he was alone. Prettyman removed her laptop computer from her briefcase and she and Davis sat down at the table for an hour, eating and making notes, offering each other suggestions in between bites of the sumptuous leftovers, as she explained the outline. They agreed that Davis should write press releases for the local papers in Los Feliz, Glendale and East Hollywood, which also were to include an invitation to residents nearby for a "Grand Reopening" of

Anna Stoddard's art gallery. In the meantime, Mary would build radio and Internet advertisement campaigns, with one-minute spots to be streamed online and broadcast on local stations.

She had done a thorough job and he was impressed with it. This was a different person than he had observed at the studio's backlot party. Her cool, icy personality was gone. She seemed at ease and relaxed, unpretentious, and even showed a sense of humor. As he walked her downstairs to her car, they agreed to meet at 9:45 the next morning at Anna Stoddard's gallery on Hillhurst Avenue.

After he'd cleaned up the kitchen, he decided to get to bed early. He turned out the small lamp on the nightstand and lay there in the dark, wondering why Patty Baker had come to his apartment. He was sure that it was her, the heavy scent of the perfume was her way of telling him so. He had to find her. Slowly, though, his thoughts shifted to Prettyman. As he drifted to sleep, he saw the light in her eyes, a radiance that, to him, would become irresistible.

Chapter 4

LEG WORK

The weather the next morning on Hillhurst Avenue was cool and overcast, the Santa Ana winds had faded out from the high desert and Rhitt Davis found a parking place for the Porsche near Anna Stoddard's art gallery. The thick marine layer drifted over the hills of Griffith Park, rising up toward the sunlight that was trying to break through, as he waited for Mary Prettyman to arrive.

The neighborhood was part of older Los Angeles, with a combination of apartment houses and red-tiled roofed two-story Spanish villas that dotted the hillside above Los Feliz Boulevard. Davis knew the area, having played golf at the Griffith Park courses during his high school summers and later from his weekend stays with Patty Baker at her apartment, nearby

Anna Stoddard's gallery was part of a quaint business district along Hillhurst that included an upscale produce store, a French restaurant, a used book store and coffee house, a bakery and a magazine and newspaper stand.

Davis lit a cigarette and watched one of the employees of the produce store, a young Middle Eastern man wearing a stained white apron, roll out and then set up stands of organic fruit that featured apples, pears, limes and bananas.

Davis heard a car approach and saw that it was Prettyman pulling up behind his 911-S in a cream-colored Nissan GT R-12 with a black cloth convertible top. She set the parking brake, opened the door and got out.

"How long have you been waiting?" she asked.

"Two or three minutes," he said as he flicked his cigarette in the gutter. She put her briefcase, a black Louis Vuitton handbag, a notepad and two ballpoint pens on the roof of the car.

"Can I help you carry some of that?"

She gestured toward the briefcase and note pads, and clicked the remote car lock.

She was dressed in a black satin blouse with three-quarter sleeves and stretch denim skinny jeans. A long, flowing cashmere sweater with a soft ruffle down the front was a perfect cover for the cool weather. Her peep-toe ankle boots revealed a rich, ruby polish on her toes that matched the color of a barrette in her hair above her right ear.

Davis grabbed the briefcase and notepads and together they walked through the entrance of Anna Stoddard's gallery.

———

Not far from Hillhurst Avenue, two miles at the most in the Hollywood Hills, Patty Baker watched Jake Dumont pace back and forth like an expectant father on the expansive redwood deck outside the sliding glass door of the recreation room at his house in Beachwood Canyon.

She lay on a chaise lounge in a black and white tankini swimsuit, dabbing a towel against her face after a brief morning workout of 10 laps in the backyard infinity pool that overlooked the Hollywood reservoir. She stood up and wrapped the towel around her waist, then returned to her reclining position, while adjusting a smaller towel around her head. She noticed beads of sweat beginning to drip from Dumont's forehead.

"Jake, sit down, you're going to have a stroke," she said.

Dumont ignored her and took a cell phone out of the pocket of his robe and dialed. Suddenly, Dumont's butler opened the sliding glass door.

"Sir, your guests are here."

Dumont put the phone back in his robe and followed the butler into the recreation room, sliding the door shut behind him.

Baker could see a tall man with a receding hairline in a dark suit talking with Dumont. He was with a woman whose back was to the patio, blocking Baker's view of her face. The woman held a dark shopping bag in her right hand.

With Dumont and the other man at her side, the woman dumped the contents of the bag onto a table. A tumble of jewelry—gold bracelets, rings and necklaces—and small objets d'art spilled out.

It appeared that at least one of the art works was a jeweled vase that had come unwrapped from its soft padded cover.

Dumont suddenly noticed Baker watching, and he gestured with his hand toward another room, ushering his guests away from the door.

Patty never intruded into Dumont's business affairs, but being left outside without even an introduction made her wonder why she bothered to stay with him. They had been introduced through a mutual friend one afternoon at the horse races at Del Mar. Dumont invited her to join him at a cocktail party that he was hosting after the ninth race. For the rest of that summer, she was on his arm at the seaside track every weekend. Then came a trip to Miami, followed by another to London.

Lately, though, the fast life of art auctions and Beverly Hills parties, more trips to Cabo San Lucas and the Bahamas and the shopping junkets to Paris and New York didn't make the everyday routine of living with him seem as exciting as it once was. The near-comatose atmosphere in the house made her wish she was somewhere else, maybe back on Rowena Avenue, in the arms of Rhitt Davis.

She used to enjoy being part of Dumont's rich and extravagant lifestyle but now the excitement of that had mostly burned up. She felt more like an expensive token, arm candy to him instead of a lover.

She got up from the chaise lounge and walked into the house through a side door, like a cleaning maid who was starting her day's work.

———

The electronic chime on the front door of Anna Stoddard's store rang as Rhitt Davis and Mary Prettyman entered the front room from the porch that faced Hillhurst Avenue. Davis closed the single glass-paneled door and the two stood in silence, soon broken by the noise of boxes sliding across the floor at the rear of what was once a small house that had its six rooms converted into to a business setting.

"Is that you, Mr. Davis?" a voice called.

"Yes, it is," Davis replied.

He and Prettyman walked down a hallway and found Anna Stoddard in a small back room sweeping up bits of broken glass and other debris. Three standing shelves had been tipped over, their contents scattered across the floor. Davis picked up several bottles of Vitamin C and Vitamin E. He righted the shelves and stood them against the wall. Davis looked at Anna's face and saw the Stoddard profile, the set jaw, the narrow distance between her dark eyes and the high forehead. She was Karl Stoddard's sister. Davis spotted a dustpan near a portrait of John Lennon and held it on the floor for Anna to sweep up the glass and dirt. She pointed to a trashcan and he emptied the contents of the pan into it.

"If I ever find out who did this they're going to regret the day they were born," Anna Stoddard said.

She leaned the broom against the wall and sat down on a chair. Mary Prettyman moved a chair from the table and sat down next to her as Davis straightened a massage table that had been pushed against the wall at an odd angle.

"Why would anyone want to hurt you and your business?" asked Prettyman.

"I don't know," Stoddard said. "I've run this gallery for six years, it is my second one, I love this area, I know everyone who comes in here, most of them are artists who live in the neighborhood." Then she laughed.

"I had a rodent problem last year, that's been the only trouble I've had, until now."

"Well, it looks like there is a different kind of rat, a two-legged one," Davis said, trying to lighten up the conversation.

Mary Prettyman stood and walked across the room. She picked up a small instrument that looked like a pen, although it had several tips, painted like the colors of the rainbow. She handed it to Anne Stoddard.

"It is my color puncture pen, the bastards," she said. "I have been offering it as treatment for various aches and pains. I was wondering what happened to it."

Davis looked at the fragments of the instrument.

"See, yellow is for intellect and digestion, blue is for calm and cooling, green helps with detoxing and letting go of stress, and red stimulates and heals."

Davis took her hand.

"The police have probably already asked you this, but did you notice anything missing, any paintings or other works that aren't here now?"

Stoddard shook her head.

"Just a couple broken port glasses, but now that you mention it, I can't find a lithograph that was in the back of the gallery. I am not sure if I gave it to somebody or what?"

"What did the lithograph look like," asked Prettyman. "Who was the artist?"

"Oh, it was a Picasso, one of dozens that he did in his later life, it was part of a set of 10 or 11 lithographs. I bought it at an auction two years ago.

"But since this trouble, business has been bad. My regular customers have stayed away. It's almost as if somebody was trying to close me down, although I can't see why anybody would want to do that."

She stopped, then said, "One thing that has had me thinking. I got two or three calls from a woman, she didn't give me her name, but she said I should stop the color puncture treatments until I could be trained and then approved by the business that officially sanctioned the practice. I hung up on her."

"Where was the woman calling from?," Davis asked.

"I don't know, Wyoming, Colorado, someplace around that part of the country."

Davis and Prettyman followed Stoddard out into the gallery.

"We have a plan that will help bring back your business," he said.

For the next 30 minutes or so, he and Prettyman sat with her and explained how Karl Stoddard and Associates would help rejuvenate Anna Stoddard's art gallery trade and health store sales.

When they had finished, she walked them out to the front of the gallery. "I sure hope you're right," she said, waiving goodbye to them as they walked up the sidewalk to their cars.

———

Rhitt Davis loaded several pieces of blank white copying paper into the Hewlett-Packard printer, and clicked PRINT from the Apple Mac Pro computer, which was located in an anteroom at Sagebrush, just down the hallway from the firm's main workroom where most the agents had their desks. The printer rolled out the first page of the press release he had written for firm's campaign to promote the grand reopening of

Anna Stoddard's art gallery.

Davis read the release, and marked a change in the second paragraph with a red pencil. As he sat back down at the computer, he saw Mary Prettyman standing in the doorway.

"I'm making a small change in this press release for the Hillhurst News. I'd like you to look it over."

As he printed a new copy, she took off her full-length, black-blue fur-collared coat and laid it on a nearby table. She leaned over his shoulder and started reading the release on the screen. He could smell her perfume, a fragrance similar to the one Patty Baker wore, but subtly different.

Davis took the copy from the printer and handed it to her.

"The one thing that bothers me is this color puncture treatment that she had started," Prettyman said. "I read up on it and most serious holistic practitioners give it mixed reviews, some even calling it a worthless treatment. I think we should stay away from it, leave it out of the release."

Davis read the press release again.

"Karl wanted it in there."

"I talked to him about it and he agreed that we just mention it at the bottom of her bio."

Prettyman put her coat on and handed the

release back to Davis and smiled. He could see again the light in her eyes.

"I'll also mention to Karl that his sister could use an updated security system. She needs something more than just a keypad and a chime on the door."

Then she added, "You did a good job on this project. I'll see you Friday at the party."

———

The small white lights strung along the front façade and on the side of Anna Stoddard's gallery flickered in the early evening dusk. Guests of the "Grand Reopening," as a large, hanging banner proclaimed, mingled near tables filled with hot and cold hors d'oeuvres. Two bartenders poured drinks at an open bar that was tucked out of sight of passing traffic on Hillhurst Avenue.

Karl Stoddard helped his sister greet many of her guests, who included old friends, Los Feliz business district neighbors and the local media. A photographer took posed and candid pictures while the circling waiters made sure that everyone had plenty to eat and drink.

An artist sat at an easel offering to draw charcoal portraits, and her generosity was getting a brisk reception. She gestured toward Rhitt Davis to sit in the chair but he smiled and shook his head, "No, thanks."

On the other side, a masseuse with a portable massage chair offered free shoulder and neck rubs to anyone who wanted them.

Davis stood near the Stoddards, and made sure that both were properly introduced to a television news reporter and her cameraman, and he encouraged her to take as much time as she needed for an interview which he hoped would be shown on the station's 11 o'clock broadcast.

Davis also kept an eye on Mary Prettyman, who curiously had stepped back from the crowd and was talking to a woman who she had invited to the party. The woman was tall and slender with long, dark hair that swept over her shoulders. She had an attractive, athletic figure and Davis noticed that she would intermittently caress Prettyman's arm.

At the right moment, Davis excused himself from the Stoddards and walked over to where Prettyman and her friend were sitting.

"Can I get you two something to drink?" he asked, gesturing toward the bar. He extended his hand toward the woman.

"I don't think we've met, my name is Rhitt Davis."

Mary stood up. "I'm sorry, I should have

introduced you earlier, this is Janie Wells, a friend from the Bay Area."

"Los Gatos, near San Jose," added Wells. "I just came down for the weekend."

She was dressed impeccably in a two-piece Navy blue silk suit with a light pink scarf that opened enough to expose a string of small pearls around her neck.

"I've played in several golf tournaments near there," Davis said. "I love that area."

They shook hands and Mary Prettyman continued.

"We were thinking about leaving soon. I've got a headache and a million things to tie up at the office next week. Do you think you can wrap things up here tonight, make sure Karl and Anna are happy with everything?"

Davis assured her that he would see that the rest of the affair would go on smoothly, and he walked both women to Prettyman's car, which was parked up the street at the curb.

Both women got into the Nissan and, with Janie Wells behind the steering wheel, the two departed for Brentwood.

Davis said "good night" and watched the car turn right on Los Feliz Boulevard. As he walked back to the party, he noticed a large gray, four-door sedan with two men inside parked on the other side of the street. It was obvious that they were watching the activities at Anna Stoddard's store.

For the rest of the evening, Davis helped bring the party to a successful conclusion. After saying goodbye to Karl Stoddard and his sister, he helped the caterer with the cleanup, and paid the waiters and bartenders in cash.

As he put on his jacket, he remembered that his cell phone was in the lower inside pocket. He took it out and saw that he had a text message. It was from Mary Prettyman. She had left her cashmere wrap and gold cigarette case inside the bar and asked if Davis could bring them by her apartment if it wasn't too much trouble. She ended the message by leaving her address and apartment number.

Davis was tired and didn't feel like driving out to the Westside of L.A. But he found the cashmere wrap and gold cigarette case tucked away on a shelf in the bar. He looked at his black-face Rolex, which read 11:45 p.m. He stared at the wrap and cigarette case again and said to himself, "What the hell."

He got into the Porsche, started the engine and drove away, not noticing that the gray four-door sedan was gone from across the street.

Chapter 5
SILK PAJAMAS
AND A STAKEOUT

Rhitt Davis knocked on Mary Prettyman's apartment door, 13E. The building was located on Chennault Street, off of Barrington Avenue, just north of San Vicente Boulevard.

He stood back from the door, listening for the sound of someone approaching from inside. He waited about a minute and just as he was considering leaving the wrap and case on the mat, the door opened revealing Janie Wells. She was wearing a long, white silk bathrobe, her hair was damp from a shower. She saw that Davis was holding Prettyman's things. Davis noted how much Wells looked like Prettyman, even with the dark hair. They could have been sisters.

"Mary forgot these at the party," he said as he held them toward her.

She gestured for him to come in and he saw Prettyman sitting on an expansive beige suede sectional sofa.

She was rubbing her temples and the back of her neck. When she saw him, she stood up and walked over, gave him a hug and took the wrap and cigarette case, setting them on a handcrafted Benchwright table near the sofa. Also on the table was an empty plastic bottle of Advil.

"Thanks for bringing these," she said. "I must have been out of it to leave a 22 karat gold case behind. Can I get you something, a drink?"

He shook his head.

"No, I'll pass. Had a couple drinks at the reception."

Janie Wells stepped between Davis and Mary. She held the empty pill bottle in the palm of her hand and Mary took it.

"I was out of Advil, you wouldn't happen to have any with you or in your car? I still have a slight headache, and if not, there's a grocery store that stays open late down at the end of the street."

"I'd do it but I'm not exactly dressed to go out," said Wells, gesturing to her hair and robe.

Davis took the bottle from Prettyman.

"I'll get some for you."

Mary walked back to the sofa, and eased her head onto one of several large eggshell-colored pillows that were spread about.

Davis walked quickly to the front door and

took the elevator down to the lobby. The doorman opened the lobby's street exit for him, and Davis told him that he wouldn't be gone long.

The night air had turned cool, with a low marine layer and cloudy mist coming onshore from Santa Monica Bay. Brentwood was barely four miles from the ocean and the low dampness hung heavy on the Westside of Los Angeles. Davis left his jacket in the Porsche, and rubbed his bare arms to warm himself. He looked at his watch as he walked along the sidewalk toward Montana Avenue. It was nearly 12:30 a.m.

About 75 yards behind him he heard a car motor start and then the sounds of a door opening and closing, followed by a scuffing of footsteps on the sidewalk. As he turned back to look he noticed a large sedan slowly pulling away from the curb.

Davis walked faster, and then broke into a full stride as he hurried to the entrance of the all-night grocery store at the corner of Barrington Avenue and San Vicente Boulevard. Inside, he quickly found the medicine section and grabbed a large bottle of Advil from the shelf. As he approached the checkout stand he saw the sedan pull into the front space of the store's parking lot.

At the cash register, a young college-aged man scanned the bottle and Davis paid for it. He glanced again at the car in the parking lot and saw the passenger door open and a man get inside the car. The young man put the bottle in a plastic bag and gave Davis a receipt.

"Is there a back way out of your store?" Davis asked.

The young man pointed to the restroom and said there was a door that opened onto an alley.

Davis thanked him, picked up the bag and walked to the rear of the store. He found the exit and quickly headed down an alley that led back toward Mary Prettyman's apartment.

When he got to her building, he waited outside and watched. Soon the same sedan that had followed him earlier made a turn onto Montana Avenue and parked in the space it had been in before. Davis was sure that it was an unmarked police car. The doorman saw him standing on the sidewalk and he opened the door. "A little cool without a jacket, Sir."

Davis answered and entered the building.

When he opened the door to her apartment he saw Mary still lying on the sofa but she had changed into a pair of pale blue silk pajamas and the light from a log fire that she had started in the fireplace flickered on the high ceiling.

He could hear her breathing as she dozed

into light sleep. Davis put the pills on the kitchen counter, found some ice in the freezer and a glass in a cupboard, which he filled with water, and carried both back to the living room, placing them on the coffee table. He adjusted the dimmer switch for the ceiling's recessed lights and brought them down to low. The room was bathed in the fire place's warm glow.

He took a blue silk afghan blanket from a large Mahogany trunk near the sofa and covered her. Davis gently put his hand on her forehead and could feel that her skin was cool. He walked over to a large picture window and peered through the side of the closed drapes. In the dark he saw the sedan re-park in a space in front of the apartment.

He stood away from the window, glanced at Prettyman as she slept, then at his watch, and again down to the street, where the man on the passenger side of the sedan had gotten out and was now standing on the sidewalk. They had to be cops, he thought, possibly the same ones that were outside Patty Baker's apartment that early morning two months earlier.

Davis wanted to go home but, after some thought, decided to stay. He was concerned for his safety and for the woman's on the couch. He stirred the burning logs with a wrought-iron poker, and took off his shirt and trousers. He spread a large wool blanket on the wood floor in front of the fireplace, took a pillow from the sofa and covered himself with a brown, wool afghan blanket. He turned on his left side toward the fire and listened to Mary's restful breathing until he fell asleep.

At 4 a.m., as the embers in the fireplace glowed, Mary Prettyman awoke, and sat up on the sofa. She rubbed her forehead and her neck and saw the glass of water on the coffee table, and took two or three sips. She looked at Davis on the floor as he slept. She leaned back against the sofa, taking more sips from the glass. The cool liquid was refreshing. Finally, she covered back up with the afghan as she lay back down.

She stared and the last remnants of the fire, then at Davis asleep on the floor. She closed her eyes for a few seconds, then opened them again and watched him as he slowly breathed. She eased herself down to the floor, unbuttoned the pearl-colored buttons of her silk top and gently pressed her breasts against his back, lightly caressing his shoulders with her fingertips.

At that moment, Janie Wells appeared from the bedroom and saw Mary and Rhitt in front of the fireplace. She wore only black lace panties.

Janie knelt behind Mary and helped her take off the silk pajama top. She kissed her and ran her hands from Prettyman's back down to her thighs.

As Davis stirred in his sleep, Mary moaned, closed her eyes and whispered to him, "I'm so glad that you are here."

————

The morning light shined through the picture window of Mary Prettyman's apartment. Rhitt Davis opened his eyes and slowly turned toward the rays. Mary watched him from the couch.

He smiled, "I can see the color in your face again."

"I never knew a glass of water could taste so good," she said.

Davis stood up, walked over to the window and peered through the open blinds to the street below. The two men and the large sedan were gone.

He looked around the spacious living room. Near the window stood a baby grand piano. Several pieces of ceramic artwork were on top of the Steinway, including dishes and bowls and cups. He picked up a cup with a long stem and held it up to the light, admiring it.

"My Beatrice Wood chalice," Mary said. "My favorite and most valuable piece in my collection."

Davis stared at a large painting on the wall near the fireplace, of a string section of a large orchestra highlighted in bright red.

"I didn't know you were this artful."

Mary watched him put the chalice back in its original spot.

"I've been playing classical piano since I was a little girl."

Davis saw that she had hung his trousers and shirt in the hallway outside her bedroom. Near the doorway on the floor were his Alfani loafers and black socks. He took his clothes from their hangers and put them on.

"I'll fix some coffee," she said as she got up from the sofa and quietly walked into the kitchen.

Davis finished dressing, then went into her bedroom and saw Janie Wells sound asleep in Mary's queen-size bed. He found the silk bathrobe that she had worn the night before. He brought it into the kitchen and wrapped it around Mary's shoulders.

"You don't want to end up in the emergency ward," he said as he helped her put her arms in the sleeves.

She smiled and went back to making the coffee.

Davis was silent for a few seconds, then asked, "Why were the police staking out your apartment last night?"

Mary filled the coffee maker with water and pushed the "On" switch.

"I want to thank you for helping me, and for all the work you did at the party last night," she said, avoiding his question.

The sound of the brewing coffee filled the kitchen. Davis looked at her. Her beautiful hazel eyes stared up into his. He was about to ask her again but she put her finger on his lips.

She opened a cupboard, took down two cups and filled both with coffee. He took a sip of the hot brew and then put down the mug.

"I've got to get my car worked on, and set up my schedule for next week."

He paused again, and said, " You need to get some rest."

Davis touched her shoulder, said goodbye, walked to the front door and let himself out.

Chapter 6
A CRIME AND OLD NEWSPAPERS

The doors to Los Angeles' downtown public library at Fifth and Hope streets, across from the Biltmore Hotel, were wide open, with two security guards on each door eyeing a stream of visitors that entered and exited the older of the library's main buildings.

Rhitt Davis followed a group of high school students to the periodical section on the second floor. He waited in line for his turn to write out a checkout request for several editions of *Herald-Examiner* news sections from the mid 1980s, when that Hearst-owned newspaper was an all-day publication in L.A. It originally was printed in the afternoon for commuters to either read on their way home on the bus, or for those who wanted to catch up on the latest news before dinner at home.

But the paper gradually lost its readership, which quickly switched to viewing television's evening news broadcasts.

Davis showed a librarian, an older woman, whom he guessed was in her early 60s, his library card. He wanted to look at microfilm of editions printed in the summer of 1986. She said that she was one of the archivists and added that her microfilm machine was being repaired, but he could try to find what he wanted in bound print editions. Davis reluctantly agreed and in a few minutes he sat at a long wooden table with two year's worth of old editions of the late newspaper.

He was looking for any story on a shooting that took place at a hilltop home in the area above the Hollywood Bowl, on or near Alta Loma Drive. Patty Baker had once mentioned that Jake Dumont was staying at a house on Alta Loma after he had gotten out of prison, and a shooting took place one night at the residence during a party. Davis remembered that Patty had said the party was outdoors so he started with the pages from the month of June.

It was a tedious chore and after about 15 minutes of turning thinly-aged pages he began to get bored with the effort, but, taking a deep breath, he kept looking, wishing the microfilm machine, which was much faster, was working.

He finally found a small story dated

August 20, 1986, whose headline read, "Gunshots Reported at Hillside Party." It was a short four-paragraph police-blotter story on the back page of the local news section that said guests at the party had heard gunshots and most of the attendees then left the party before the police arrived. Apparently no one was hurt but what caught Davis' eye was that the party's host was none other than Maurice Otto.

Davis wondered if this may have been the same party that Patty Baker had told him about. The question was, was it Otto's house or was he using it to host the party? In any case, Dumont and Otto's paths may have crossed that night, and where did the mysterious gunshots come from?

Davis thumbed through a few more pages of the paper to check for any other reports of the incident, but finding none he told the archivist that he had finished with the bound editions. He helped her put them back in their wooden cabinets and made a note to find out when Karl Stoddard had taken on Maurice Otto as a client.

Noticing it was after one, he crossed Fifth Street to the Bunker Hill Spanish steps and hiked up to one of his favorite restaurants, McCormick and Schmick's. The longtime L.A. eatery in the financial district attracted a lunch brigade of lawyers, bankers and downtown brokerage firm workers. It was also one of Stoddard's hangouts when he had a business meeting at the firm's downtown office in the U.S. Bank tower. Davis sat down at a small table in the bar and ordered the menu's seafood platter and a glass of ice tea. He noticed a *LIFE* magazine cover photograph of Lana Turner hanging in a frame on a wall near his table. Davis stared at the picture of the glamorous actress, whom he remembered starring in the movie, *The Postman Always Rings Twice*, and how much she looked like an actress he had seen in recent films. As Davis ate his lunch, he stared at Turner's face and tried to recall who she reminded him of.

He finished the seafood dish, which included salmon, crab cakes and sand dabs. He drank his iced tea and was about to pay the tab when his cell phone rang. He picked it up from the table.

"This is Rhitt Davis. "

"Rhitt, where are you?"

Davis recognized Patty Baker's voice.

"I am downtown. I'm just finishing up lunch."

"Can you meet me at Union Station?" she asked. "I am leaving town on the 2:20 train to Chicago. I have to talk to you before I go."

Chapter 7
A KISS AND A WARNING

Rhitt Davis hurried down the Spanish Steps of the Library Tower plaza. He ran across Hope Street on the green light and walked quickly toward the subway entrance at the Pershing Square station.

Davis bought a $1.50 ticket and waited two minutes for the Red Line train to Union Station. The Red Line subway, which began its journey to downtown from North Hollywood in the San Fernando Valley, rolled into the station from the dark tunnel and Davis stepped aboard. He saw a seat in the rear of the train but elected to stand when a woman with a small child in a stroller boarded after him.

The train moved forward and picked up speed as it left Pershing Square. Only one stop, at the Hill Street station, remained before its final destination. After the stop at Hill Street, the train rolled again, but came to a slow crawl as it crossed over tracks that led to the boarding platform at Union Station. Davis looked at his watch and swore under his breath. He was going to miss her if the train didn't pick up some speed. Why was it slowing down?

Suddenly, though, the train lunged forward and Davis held on to a stainless steel pole to keep his balance. With his other hand he removed a linen handkerchief from his back pocket and wiped the sweat off his forehead as he stared out the window at the darkness of the tunnel. He could see the reflection of his taut profile in the glass window of the car as the tunnel started to turn from dark to light.

The Red Line train began to slow again as it rolled to a stop. The automated doors opened and Davis inched his way forward, then bolted out, dodging past passengers who were exiting the car.

He ran to an escalator and climbed the steps two at a time until halfway when he had to squeeze past a group of people with suitcases. When he reached the top, he turned right and walked into the old station's main concourse.

It was a huge, ornate room filled mostly with large, comfortable chairs. Iron and glass chandeliers hung from a high wood-beam ceiling. Spanish-style windows offered picturesque views of the outside of the terminal, including a restaurant's spacious patio and fountains in a plaza. Rays of the setting sun reflected on a red-tile floor.

Davis hurried to a digital directory that listed departure times. He scanned the board for trains that were schedule to leave at 2:20 p.m., and saw that the Zephyr for Chicago was in its last boarding call.

He walked quickly past a tour group of senior citizens who were listening to a lecture given by a docent about the history of the station. He saw several commuters relaxing in a corner bar, chatting away about their day at work while asking a busy bartender if they could have another glass of wine before it was time to depart.

A homeless black man walked slowly past, holding out a cup in his hand for spare coins for what he said was for a telephone call he needed to make.

And an attractive, well-dressed woman flagged down a security officer to report that she had been harassed by a man who had followed her from the parking lot.

Davis hurried to platform 7B, and walked up the inside of the ramp, past a stream of arriving passengers. He stopped at the top and looked around. The blue and white Amtrak to Chicago was ready to go. Suddenly, from above the din of the train's idling motors, he heard a woman's voice call his name.

"Rhitt."

He turned around and there was Patty Baker. She walked up to him, put down her travel bag and put her arms around his shoulders.

She softly said, "Hello, Player."

She kissed his lips then buried her head into his neck, lightly rubbing her lips against it as she started to cry.

"What's going on?" Davis asked. "You've got to tell me, Patty, you haven't got much time."

She took a tissue out of her purse and wiped her eyes.

"I am so scared. All I know is somebody has given Jake a lot of money and it's not from gambling. It's not from his fucking film business, either. A man has been staying at the house. He's German or Czech, or Eastern European, I don't know. But a couple nights ago I walked into the living room—"

"At the house in Beachwood Canyon?" Davis asked, interrupting her.

"He's got two, this one is farther up the hill. This guy was on the phone with somebody and he was translating his conversation for Jake. When Jake saw me he went nuts, he hit me and threatened to kill me if I said anything. He also told me to stay away from you."

He pushed aside her hair and saw a yellowing bruise on the side of her forehead. She put the tissue in the pocket of her wool jacket.

Davis looked at her, then asked "Did you come over to my apartment, go inside?"

"Yes, but you weren't home. I was worried that somebody had followed me so I left, drove back to the other house."

Davis was silent for a few seconds, then asked her, "Where are you going to stay in Chicago?"

"I've got a girlfriend who lives in Lake Forest. I can stay with her as long as I want.

"Rhitt, you've got to be careful."

Davis took her into his arms and held her.

"Why did you ever have to get involved with a guy like Dumont?"

She looked up into his eyes.

"I'm sorry. It hasn't been good for either one of us, has it?"

As he held her, she pushed the inside of her thigh against his and tightly held it there. She kissed him again, then picked up her bag and walked to the steps of the passenger car. A conductor helped her up.

The train slowly began to move forward and in a minute or so, it was gone out of sight.

Chapter 8
OUT OF BOUNDS

It was the Monday before Christmas and as sometimes happens late in the year, L.A. was hit by a
heat-wave, but this one was humid and damp
making the air heavy, the remnants of a tropical
storm that had moved north along the Southern
California coast from Baja, Mexico.

Rhitt Davis thought it was odd that Maurice
Otto wanted to play golf with the holiday just a
few days away. He couldn't have been that eager
for a rematch. On the other hand, Otto was Jewish,
so he probably didn't care that much about cele-
brating Christmas.

When Davis drove through the entrance of
the Wilshire Club, he expected the parking lot to
be empty because the club was usually closed on
Mondays for maintenance, or sometimes a charity
golf tournament. But the parking area was full of
cars, he could see a lot of activity in the clubhouse,
and players ready to tee off on the first hole.

Of course, he remembered, it was the club

members' Christmas party. And, the course was open. Davis entered the front door and walked past the celebration, his golf clubs slung over his shoulder. He waived to a member that he knew, who called back to him

"Hey, Rhitt, it's Christmas, join us for a drink."

Davis smiled, waived and said, "Later," and kept walking, making it to the expansive veranda where he saw Otto and another man in the distance standing on the edge of the first tee next to two golf carts. As he approached them, he immediately recognized the one standing next to Maurice Otto. It was Jake Dumont.

Otto introduced Davis to Dumont and the two men shook hands. Dumont wasn't as tall as the man Davis had seen in the gallery photos in the downtown library, a bit under six feet three, and not as slim, with added weight settling over his belly. Dumont's hands trembled slightly and he self-consciously kept one either in his pocket or behind his back.

"You had quite a basketball career," Davis said as he put his clubs on the back end of one of the carts. "Averaged nearly 15 points a game, I think."

Dumont stared at Davis.

"Mr. Davis, you're not old enough to have seen me play basketball. That was back in the late

1970s, you had to be in kindergarten," Dumont said laughing, as he glanced at Otto.

Davis replied, "I used to get paid for knowing statistics like that."

Maurice Otto informed Dumont that Davis had a newspaper background and once worked in a sports department.

"Maurice, I thought you said Mr. Davis was in public relations. What sports did you cover?" Dumont asked.

Davis unzipped his golf bag and took out his golf shoes. As he put them on, he said, "Mostly golf, and some basketball. You're right, your playing days were before my time."

Davis removed the cover from his driver, took a two or three practice swings. Because he was the oldest of the three, Otto claimed first-to-hit honors, saying, "Shall we make it $1,000 a hole?"

Davis stopped swinging his club. Maurice Otto had never played for more than $100 a hole since Karl Stoddard had set up their first golf date.

Dumont waited for Davis to answer.

"The kosher food business must be doing well," Davis said.

"Hell, I wish," he answered. "Since I last saw you, I've partnered up with Mr. Dumont in his end of the film business.

As Davis watched Otto tee up his ball, he chuckled to himself. "So, Maurice is now in the xxx-rated section of the movie theater."

Dumont was next to hit. He took an unorthodox swing at the ball, standing on his toes as he took the club away in his back swing, then lunged, striking it hard at the heel of the club-face, and sent it skyward in an arching fade to the right where it landed among three trees. Dumont slammed the club on the ground, and then jammed it into his golf bag.

Davis addressed his ball and sent his tee shot left of center down the fairway.

After they had finished the fifth hole, Davis was ahead by $5,000 and it was evident that if he played his steady game he would win all 18 holes.

As the afternoon progressed toward evening, muggy storm clouds gathered and the skies darkened. The sound of thunder could be heard to the southwest. There was a good chance that it would start raining before the threesome had finished.

After the group teed off on the 11th hole, Davis pulled his cart along side Otto and Dumont.

"Maurice, if we start getting wet, do you want to continue?"

"Damn it, Davis, we're down $10,000 each.

You're not quitting because of a little rain," Otto shouted.

Davis heard Dumont say, "Relax Maurice, we have time."

The trio reached the 12th green, the farthest point on the course from the clubhouse. The only other people in sight were gardeners, mostly Latino men and women, who were busy on their hands and knees planting flowers and pulling up weeds along the edges of a fence that separated the backyards of several stately homes of Hancock Park from the Wilshire Club's fairways.

One of the women, dressed in khaki pants, a flowing blue denim shirt and wearing a wide-brimmed straw sun hat watched Davis, Dumont and Otto putt out. She lowered her head and went back to work, digging shallow holes with a small trowel and dropping in Zinnia and Cosmos seeds with her bare hands. She covered the seeds with dirt, patting the soil down. The gold and silver rings on her fingers became caked with mud as she kneaded the soil until she was satisfied with the planting. She adjusted a sterling silver wristband with a blue topaz stone in the center higher up under the sleeve of her shirt.

Then she took a small sprinkling can and watered the seeds. As she did this she glanced up to see Otto strike the fender of the cart with his putter, frustrated at losing another hole. From her spot along the fence line, Mary Prettyman watched the group then drive over to the 13th tee box.

Suddenly, two men who looked like groundskeepers drove past Prettyman in a flatbed electric work cart and they followed Davis, Dumont and Otto down the 13th fairway, which was a dog-leg left. Otto's drive had gone into the woods just off the left-hand side and into a grove of Oak and Sycamores trees. As Davis helped Otto search for his ball, the two men pulled up alongside them. Davis guessed that they were going to help look, too, but instead they quickly approached Davis, grabbed him by the shirt and threw him to the ground.

Davis struggled to get to his feet, pushing aside one of the men. "What's the big idea," he shouted.

The second man, a burly Hispanic, raised his fist and hit Davis on the chin with a straight right-hand punch. He fell unconscious nearly hitting his head on the side of the golf cart.

———

Darkness had come and a light rain had left the air sticky and damp. A numbing pain in his jaw and a pair of bright lights in his face brought Rhitt Davis back to consciousness. He tried to walk but his legs wouldn't move. He shook his head to regain his senses and realized that his feet and hands were bound to a tree.

The bright beams came from the two headlights of the gardeners' flatbed electric cart. Davis could make out the shadowy outlines of two men standing near the lights. Gradually he began to feel a burning sensation between his legs—an athletic supporter. It had been placed tightly around his groin, he was naked, his clothes cast in the rough nearby.

"Sorry the jock strap isn't your size, Mr. Davis. Next time we'll get the right one."

Davis recognized Jake Dumont's voice. He heard the other man laugh.

"You might be feeling a little uncomfortable around the family jewels. It's an old practical joke that the seniors used to pull on the undergrads during training camp. Soak their jockstraps with Ben-Gay ointment and pretty soon their balls feel like they are on fire."

More laughter assaulted Davis' throbbing head.

"But I'll give you a chance to get out of this, alive. All you have to tell me is where Patty Baker is."

Davis was silent for few seconds, then answered

as he tried to spread his legs apart.

"What makes you think I know where she is?"

"We both know the answer to that question," Mr. Davis. He could hear the anger building in Dumont's voice.

"Well, I'll say this to you Jake. Maybe there was a time when I would tell you. After all, she left me for you, and that put me in a bad way, so why should I care what happens to her?

"But after reading and hearing about what a jerk you are, and now finally meeting you, and realizing all the hearsay is true, yeah, I know where she is."

Dumont waited. The night air was filled with the sounds of crickets and an occasional car passing on nearby Beverly Blvd.

"Besides being a jerk, you're a lousy golfer. Where is Maurice?"

Dumont was seething.

"Otto has decided to pick up. You see this man here, I think after you spend some time with him, you'll be more than glad to tell me where she is."

In the beams of the headlights, Davis squinted to see a middle-aged man, about five feet ten inches tall, step in front of Dumont.

Dumont gritted his teeth. "Make him talk."

The man walked up to Davis and stopped,

no more than six inches from his face. Davis guessed he was in his mid-50s with slight build and receding hairline. He handed his jacket to Dumont. He took a large Buck knife from the inner breast pocket.

"My name is Cariso. This is a 7-inch Buck knife, among the finest of all hunting knifes. I can draw and quarter a full-sized male deer with it in one hour."

He ran the tip of the knife from Davis' forehead, down his left cheek. A bead of sweat followed the point to Davis' chin.

"Have you ever heard the phrase "death by a thousand cuts?"

Davis was silent.

"It's an ancient Chinese form of torture where the victim bleeds to death from precise cuts made all over the body. The ritual usually starts with the eyes but I think we'll save those for now so that you can watch the procedure, watch the blood drain from your body."

He ran the point of the Buck knife along Davis' forehead, only this time the knife cut into the skin. Blood immediately ran down the side of Davis' face.

Dumont stepped forward. "Time's running out, Davis. Tell me where Patty Baker is."

Dumont's voice was so loud that he did not hear the crunch of a leaf underfoot about 10 yards behind them.

In the dark, Mary Prettyman crouched behind the trunk of a large Sycamore tree. From her beige gardening bag she found a pair of gloves and put them on. Then she took a Glock 23, .45 caliber semi-automatic pistol, standard FBI issue, from the bag along with a 9-millimeter silencer. She quickly screwed the silencer into the threaded barrel of the gun, switched on the pistol's red laser light and aimed the beam at Cariso.

Prettyman fired two quick shots. The first bullet struck Cariso in the back of the right leg, blowing his kneecap out onto the ground several feet away while severing the anterior crucial and Miniscus ligaments.

The second bullet ripped into Cariso's left hamstring, cutting it like a surgeon's scalpel. The muscle snapped like a rubber band leaving his leg dangling at an odd angle.

Cariso screamed as he fell to the ground, the Buck knife falling at Davis' feet.

The burly Hispanic man stared at the figure writhing on the grass, then bolted into the darkness like a startled deer. A stunned Dumont snapped out of his stupor and ran for the groundskeepers' cart, jumped in and floored the accelerator. The tires skidded in a patch of dirt, kicking up a cloud of dust. Dumont pointed the cart to the fairway and drove as fast as he could back toward the clubhouse.

As thunder and heat lightning passed overhead, Davis saw the Buck knife. His bonds were loose enough to slip his hands from the ropes. He grabbed the knife and cut his legs free.

He stood over Cariso. "You'll live pal, but you'll need to buy a walker."

Davis cut the jock strap from his waist and put on his clothes, cinching his belt buckle tight and ran up the course's cart path to the clubhouse.

As he approached the gate to the parking lot, Davis saw a golf cart parked at an odd angle just off the the fairway path. He noticed that there was a man sitting on the driver's side and as Davis got closer he recognized Maurice Otto, who was slumped over on the seat, unconscious. Davis could see a welt protruding on his forehead and spots of blood on his shirt. Feeling Otto's pulse, he was satisfied that the old man was just knocked out.

Davis' golf bag and clubs were still strapped to the back of the cart. He slung the bag's strap over his shoulder and hurried to the parking lot, where his pickup truck still sat in Karl Stoddard's slot, the only vehicle in the lot. He put the clubs in the back of the truck, started the motor and drove out to Larchmont Avenue turning left toward Hollywood.

———

The night air was still thick and damp as Rhitt Davis eased himself into the redwood hot-tub, which sat on the roof of his flat, high above Franklin Avenue. Davis sighed as the jets of water bubbled over the lower part of his body. Far off to the east, past the skyscrapers of downtown L.A., he could see lightning flicker in the heavens and heard the distant sound of thunder roll across the basin.

He tenderly ran his index finger along the cut on his forehead. The bleeding had stopped, but the wound was swollen and seeping. He considered calling the police and reporting the attack at the golf course. He hesitated, though, because he didn't want to drag Patty Baker back to Jake Dumont or his cronies.

Davis sat on the tub's bench and leaned back against the wooden edge, his arms outstretched.

As he closed his eyes, he heard footsteps coming up the stairs to the roof. He glanced over to the doorway and saw Mary Prettyman standing under the rooftop light. She was still dressed in her khaki trousers and long-sleeved blue denim shirt. She walked over to Davis and saw the cut on his face.

"I was in the area so I thought I drop by. Your door was open."

She gestured with her hand to his forehead. "What happened?"

"Oh, I met a couple guys on the golf course who wanted to use my face as a carving board. That was after they wrapped my nuts with an analgesic."

Davis adjusted himself on the hot tub seat.

Mary moved closer to look at the cut. "Do you have a bottle of antiseptic?"

Davis pointed to the door. "In the bathroom."

Prettyman walked quickly down the stairs and returned about five minutes later. She had taken off her clothes and wrapped herself in a large bath towel. In both hands she managed to carry pieces of cotton, a small tube of Neosporin, a bottle of hydrogen peroxide, and two cocktail glasses—a bourbon and soda for herself and a gin and tonic for Davis, with a slice of lime.

She found a small plastic table near the edge of the tub and set the drinks down. Then she set the cotton, Neosporin and the brown plastic bottle of hydrogen peroxide on the patio deck next to the tub. She undid her towel, letting it drop to the ground, and swung her leg over the edge of the redwood tub, lowering herself directly onto Davis' lap in the bubbling water..

Davis watched in amazed silence as she settled into the water facing him.

She carefully soaked the cotton with hydrogen peroxide and dabbed it along the open wound. Davis winced as she wiped away a few traces of blood. Then she smeared Neosporin from one end of the cut to the other

"You're lucky, I don't think it will scar. When was the last time you had a tetanus shot?"

"Oh, I don't know, maybe Fourth Grade."

"Get another ASAP."

Prettyman put the cotton back on the cement deck next to the tub, then massaged Davis' shoulders. He ran his hands slowly up and down her sides and she leaned forward and kissed him.

Davis whispered, "What, no trifecta tonight?"

Mary shook her head. "Janie's gone back to San Jose."

She slid off his lap and sat down on the bench next to him. He gave her room and put his arm around her shoulders as she rested her head on his chest. They both looked up at the sky as a few drops of rain caressed their faces. He held her close as she ran her hand over his thighs and stomach.

"Well, I hope all the parts are still in working order," she said smiling as she kissed him again.

Davis noticed that her fingernails had dirt underneath them.

"I suppose you want to know where Patty Baker is too?"

"Yes," Mary Prettyman sighed. "But not right now, not until morning."

Chapter 9
MARY'S REVELATION

The rain made the sound of a gentle patter on the patio and Rhitt Davis opened the sliding glass door to his redwood deck to let the cooler air into the kitchen. He went back to cooking breakfast for himself and Mary Prettyman, who had filled a cocktail tumbler with Windex and was gently soaking her gold rings and bracelet in the cleanser to rid them of the dirt from the gardens of the Wilshire Club golf course.

Davis wore a pair of white tennis shorts as he served her a healthful breakfast of poached egg on sourdough toast, black coffee and fig yogurt. She fanned herself with her hand and unbuttoned the front of an old polo shirt that she had found in Davis' bedroom closet after she had showered.

"Doesn't seem like Christmastime with this sticky weather," she said as she sipped her coffee.

Davis sat down at the table next to her and ate his breakfast. She watched him eat, and then she whispered softly, her wet lips brushing his earlobe, "You're too cool for your own good."

"Why do you say that?"

"You were going to let that guy cut your balls off last night before telling him where your friend, or is it ex-friend, Ms. Baker is. Why the long-suffering loyalty?"

"For me, she's not that easy to forget."

"You're going to make me beg for it, aren't you?"

Davis looked at her. Mary Prettyman was even more beautiful without makeup. She took her gold rings and bracelet out of the tumbler and walked over to the sink. She pulled the stopper and rinsed off her jewelry in warm water, blotting it dry before she put them on her fingers and left wrist.

Davis stood up and walked over to the counter and turned on small radio. The station was set on an all-news broadcast station, and the announcer was reporting on the assault of Maurice Otto.

"The 75-year-old Otto was found in his car early this morning by an employee of the Wilshire Club. Police said that Mr. Otto, who owns a nationwide chain of delicatessens and is on the board of directors of Enterprise Pictures here in Hollywood, appeared to have been injured on the golf course and had spent the night in his car."

Davis lowered the volume on the radio and raised his eyebrows. He hoped that Maurice would keep what happened on the golf course to himself and not go to the police.

He returned to his chair and Prettyman wrapped her bare leg around his under the table. He put his hand down and caressed her thigh.

"How much does Karl Stoddard know about you? I am guessing but I don't think you came to L.A. just for public relations?"

She unwrapped her leg from around Davis' and sat back. She told him that she had done some informant work for the FBI in the past and that the Bureau wanted specific information on Jake Dumont, that Dumont had come in contact, on at least three occasions, with a German naturopath named Johannes Frieder, who headed an organization of homeopathic clinics in India, Western Europe and the United States that specialized in an acupuncture-related treatment called color puncture, which Frieder claimed he invented.

Before that, the FBI wasn't that concerned with Dumont's gambling, his association with the pornographic film industry or his oriental art trading with the Chinese.

But Johannes Frieder was different. After the

subway bombings in London in 2003, English intelligence determined that there was a possible connection between Frieder and a terrorist cell in Germany, that an underground network had funneled money from Frieder's clinics to the cell, and that Frieder entities in India may be connected with an anti-Pakistani government group, whose sole intent was to undermine relations with the United States.

"When I saw that colored-light pen on the floor of Anna Stoddard's clinic, her story about the phone calls made sense that whomever was breaking into her store was trying to shut down her business."

The buzzer on the dryer in Davis' laundry porch sounded and Prettyman got up to retrieve her freshly washed clothes.

She took off the polo shirt and handed it to Davis, then put on the blue work shirt and trousers.

"It is clear that Frieder wants a lock on the worldwide color puncture market. Anyone offering the service other than his attendants could end up like Anna Stoddard."

As she slipped her leather belt through the loops, she continued, "When the Bureau found out that your Ms. Baker was Dumont's mistress and that you knew her, it opened a door for us to approach her. We explained our concern to Karl Stoddard and he agreed to let me come to work at the firm."

"And?" Davis asked

"And your government is seeking your cooperation to help find her. She probably knows things about Dumont that the Bureau would need. We believe that Frieder visited Dumont at his house in Beachwood Canyon recently, and that Patty Baker was there."

Mary Prettyman looked at Davis.

"There is the possibility here that peoples' lives are at stake. That is, as you asked, what is really going on, at least up to now."

Davis glared at her. "You're using me to get to her."

Mary Prettyman could hear the sudden distrust in Rhitt Davis' voice.

"Believe me, my feelings for you are real and I'm trying to keep them from having any influence on my job."

She wiped her eyes with her fingers and finished getting dressed.

Davis walked to the open doorway to the patio and stared at the raindrops as they hit the redwood slats.

He turned back and saw her tying the laces of

her work boots.

"What are you going to do now?"

"Dumont has recently purchased a ranch near Santa Paula, I was going to drive up there today and take a look around."

Davis put his arms around her and held her close. "Patty Baker is in the Chicago area, she said Lake Forest. She told me that she feared for her life and that she was leaving Dumont."

Mary Prettyman squeezed Davis' arm tightly.

"Would you like to ride along with me?"

"OK, I'll drive. Give me a couple minutes to change."

———

Rhitt Davis slowly guided his Ford F-150 pickup truck off the road and stopped under the shade of a large Oak tree. He set the hand brake in place and turned off the motor. Mary Prettyman studied a map on her tablet, which she plugged into the dashboard cigarette lighter, then opened the door and got out of the truck. She walked up the road for about 50 yards and stopped, looked at the open land off to the right side of the highway, then walked back to the Ford and got in.

"Drive up another mile or so. I think we're getting close."

Davis started the motor and headed back

onto Highway 126, the main road that connected the outskirts of L.A.'s north valley with the fringe of the Ojai coastal mountains.

The stark vastness of the land was broken by groves of orange trees and newly planted rows of strawberries that would be ready for harvest in the late spring, and tarp-covered stands selling fresh vegetables and fruit were perched along the side of the road. Migrant families with pickup trucks like Davis' waved to Rhitt and Mary, showing off ripe slices of watermelon and cantaloupe as they rode past.

Davis had driven for another five minutes when Mary held up her hand. "Hold it, here."

The truck pulled over and as it stopped she jumped out, slung her gardening bag over her shoulder, then turned back to Davis. She took a pistol out of the bag and handed it to him.

"What am I supposed to do with this,?" he asked."

"Probably, nothing, but if you have to use it, aim and pull the trigger."

He watched her walk quickly along the side of the highway, up a rise and then over it. She walked down the other side and disappeared from his view. He got out of the truck and started to walk after her but stopped, and decided to stay where he was.

The highway was deserted, except for an occasional 18-wheeler that roared by, bound on the inland route for Ventura or maybe Santa Barbara.

Mary walked up to an old brown-colored telephone pole, took a rope from her bag and tossed it around the first metal foot-hold, and pulling herself up, climbed to the top where the telephone wires were attached to the T-bar that crossed the pole. From that height, she could see a sprawling California-style Ranch house about a quarter of a mile away that was surrounded by citrus and avocado orchards. A long dirt driveway ran from the highway to the main house and separated it from a large guesthouse and parking breezeway that was covered by a wood-shingle roof. On the very north end of the property there was a landing strip suitable for a private plane to land and take off on.

Mary took a standard listening surveillance coil from her gardening bag and attached it to the telephone wire.

Meanwhile, Davis leaned against the side of his truck and waited for her. As he watched the road he heard a scratching noise near the back. He walked to the rear and peeked around the right fender, and saw a small black dog lift its leg and pee on the tire.

"Hey, what do you think you're doing, you mutt?"

The dog looked at Davis and ran toward the front of the truck. Davis followed, only to see the dog stop at the open passenger door and jump into the pickup.

Davis hurried back to the driver's side and laughed when he saw the dog sitting in the middle of the front seat.

Up ahead, Mary finished attaching the coil to the wire, which would allow a listener to overhear calls on the landline and cellphone from inside the house. Then, as she started to climb down the pole, she saw two men get into a late-model Mercedes-Benz and head up the dirt driveway toward her.

She quickly climbed down to the lowest foothold, grabbed the rope and lowered herself to the ground. She ran as fast as she could back to Davis and when she saw him she yelled, "Let's get out of here."

Davis saw her and yelled back, "There's a dog in the truck."

"What?"

Mary Prettyman got into the truck and slammed the door. She saw the small black canine on the seat and she smiled as she picked it up, holding it as she slid onto the floor under the dashboard.

Davis got in and started the motor. He put Mary's broad-rimmed sunhat on his head and turned away as the Mercedes went passed. The car didn't stop. He waited until it was about a quarter of a mile behind them, then stomped on the truck's accelerator, sending it back to the highway in the opposite direction. Mary sat on the floor and the little dog licked her face.

Davis got the truck up to nearly 60 miles per hour, then suddenly pulled off the road and slammed on the brakes.

"We've got a new friend," Mary said, as she sat up on the seat.

"We're not taking the dog with us," Davis said.

"Why not? I can feel his little ribs, he hasn't been eating."

Davis shook his head. "It's got a collar, it belongs to somebody."

Mary felt the collar, which was worn and faded.

"I think this little guy has been on his own for some time, and abused too, look, he's got a burn mark on his leg."

"What kind of a dog is it? Whose dog is it?"

Mary set the back legs on her lap. Davis could see it was mostly black, but had a bit of white fur on its chest.

"I think it's a mix, it might have some Yorkie or Schipperke in it. Such a sweet face," said Mary as she smoothed the fur under the dog's eyes with her thumb. She had completely forgotten about the wiretap.

Davis looked out the back window of the truck toward the highway.

"Look, we can't take it with us."

Mary stared at Davis, then back at the dog. "I'm going to bring him home with me. That's Jake Dumont's house down there and those guys are going to be back."

Davis set his jaw tight, let out a deep breath and gave in. He drove the truck back onto Highway 126.

As they headed west to the state highway, she put the dog on the seat between herself and Davis. He looked at her, then at the dog and they both started to laugh.

"That was a close one," said Mary.

Davis nodded. "Yes we nearly bogeyed that hole."

Mary sat up, looked at Rhitt, then at the dog.

"Bogey, that might be a good name for him, don't you think?"

"I'd prefer a birdie than a bogey."

She took the dog in her arms, leaned her head back on the top of the seat and closed her eyes.

For the next hour, Davis drove the coastal road back to the city, and using surface streets, arrived at Mary's apartment as the storm passed to the East and a sunset painted the western sky.

———

Christmas Day came and in the early morning, Rhitt Davis arrived at Mary Prettyman's apartment with gifts for her and Bogey. In the three days since they'd found the dog, Mary had fattened up the little black ball with ground beef, doggie biscuits and plenty of water and love.

Two visits to the Brentwood veterinarian clinic had produced a battery of vaccinations, grooming and the implanting of two digital chips, one for identification and the other for global positioning.

The vet estimated that the dog was around three years old and had been on its own for several days, probably let out of car a along the highway, and was lucky not to have been killed by a coyote or a raccoon.

Before the chips were surgically inserted

between the dog's shoulder blades, the vet asked Mary what was the dog's name? She hesitated, then said, "His name is Bogey . . . yes, Bogey."

Now, on this Christmas morning Davis brought a dog brush and treats in Christmas wrapping paper for Bogey and present for Mary wrapped in gold paper and ribbon. She opened it and inside was a wooden handmade brush and comb from Saks Fifth Avenue.

"I wanted both of you to look your best," he said.

Mary kissed him and said she had something for him. From under a small Christmas tree on the piano she took a box and he opened it. Inside were the bottoms of dark blue silk pajamas.

"I have the top," she said. "Merry Christmas, Rhitt."

Mary added that she had finally gotten a good night sleep the night before after two nights of Bogey whimpering and getting used to his new home. She asked Davis if he would watch the dog for a couple days while she visited Janie Wells in San Jose.

"You mean take the dog over to my apartment?"

"It's only for two days, then I'm coming back and Janie is flying down for New Year's. And, I think it's a good idea to stay with Bogey here because another strange place would only confuse him."

Mary kissed Davis again. "Also, I don't think you are safe over in Hollywood."

She walked over to an antique desk, opened the top drawer and took out the pistol that she had given him on the trip to Santa Paula.

"Put this in your golf bag. I'll feel a lot better knowing you've got some protection."

She ran her index finger along the cut on his forehead which had nearly healed. "You know what I mean?"

Mary spent the rest of the morning packing a leather-bound carry-on suitcase and getting dressed for her trip. She looked gorgeous in flowing white St. John trousers topped by a wide leather belt, a long-sleeved see-through light blue lace blouse and her full-length fur coat. Davis drove her to Hollywood Airport in Burbank. Bogey sat between them in the front seat of the pickup truck, wearing his new brown and blue plaid Burberry collar with matching leash attached.

The traffic was heavy so Davis drove the truck to the drop-off zone in front of the Southwest Airlines terminal. Mary opened the door and he watched her get out. She turned around to face him and he saw a cold and distant look in her eyes, the likes of which he had not seen before.

"You two stay out of trouble."

She stared at him, and said, "I will call you."

She closed the door and he watched her walk to the entrance until a traffic cop motioned for him to move on. He tried to see her out in his rear-view mirror but she had disappeared into the crowded terminal.

———

Davis spent the rest of the day delivering presents to friends, including a stop at Sagebrush where Karl Stoddard was hosting a small party for staff and family. Davis showed off Bogey, who instantly became the delight of the party, and he was pleased to see Stoddard smile at him, for a change, when he gave him tickets to a play that was opening at the Music Center.

He and Bogey arrived back at Mary Pretty-man's apartment in the early evening, and after taking the dog for a walk, Davis watched television until he fell asleep on her bed.

About an hour later, he was awakened by the kitchen telephone. He estimated that it had rung five or six times before he groggily stumbled out of the bedroom to answer it.

"Hello," Davis said.

A woman's voice answered, "This is Janie Wells, Rhitt. Is Mary there?"

An icy streak of dread shot down Davis' spine. He instantly saw the strange look on Mary's face when she said goodbye.

The concern in Janie Wells' voice was genuine. She said Mary had not arrived at her house at the time she was expected. Mary was almost 11 hours overdue.

Davis told Janie not to worry and that he would call her back. He quickly got dressed, and was about to leave when he remembered the gun and the dog. Bogey was awake and Davis found his leash, put it on his collar and the two headed down to the exit of the apartment building.

Chapter 10
TOO CLOSE AND NO COMFORT

Despite the warning that Mary Prettyman had given him, Rhitt Davis felt safer in his own apartment. He knew its surroundings, which included the neighbors, people who he saw going to work everyday and he could use it as his base of operations. And, the fact that Mary was apparently missing made him feel uncomfortable sleeping in her bed alone.

Twenty-four hours had passed since he dropped her at the airport and she still hadn't shown up at Janie Wells' house in San Jose.

Bogey had been pacing the hardwood floor in Davis' living room, so Davis joined him. The two walked the length of the room to its vista windows, then back toward the entrance.

"What do you think?" Davis said looking down at the black dog. Bogey looked up at Davis, wagged his tale and barked.

"I agree. Even though she's not where she said

she would be I don't think she's in harm's way."

Davis decided to call Sagebrush and when Joyce Myers, Karl Stoddard's secretary, answered the phone, he wished her a Happy New Year and asked if Mary was in the office.

"She's taking some vacation, Rhitt, then she's due back for a meeting with a new client, but not till after the 2nd," Randolph said.

———

Rhitt Davis lit a cigarette and stared out of the large picture window in his living room at the emerging lights of the city. He took a long drag on the Winston and then exhaled, blowing the smoke toward the ceiling.

It had been two days since he last saw Mary Prettyman at the airport. Davis took another long drag on the cigarette. The distant look on her face and the sight of her walking toward the terminal were both vivid pictures in his mind.

He turned and saw Bogey sitting patiently, looking at him.

"Where do you think she is?" Davis asked.

Bogey wagged his small tail and barked.

"Really, you know?"

Bogey barked again. Davis heard his cell phone ringing and he walked into the kitchen to answer it.

"Rhitt Davis here."

He recognized the voice on the other end as Gardens of Tasco assistant manager Angel Campos's. "Senor Rhitt, I thought I'd call you. Jake Dumont just walked into the restaurant."

Davis thanked Campos and clicked his cell phone off. He grabbed his jacket and headed down the stairwell to his car.

———

Davis let the restaurant's valet park the Porsche. He put on his jacket and hurried to the entrance where he was greeted by Campos, who had a concerned look on his face.

"Senor Rhitt, wait." He put his hand out to stop Davis.

"No trouble, please. Come with me."

Davis followed Campos through the kitchen and into a small office just off the main dining room. The office had a second door that opened onto the corner of the dining area. In the door was a small window. Campos motioned for Davis to look out onto the dining room's guests.

Davis surveyed several occupied tables. When he saw who was seated in a booth in the dimly-lit corner his heart jumped. There was Jake Dumont and leaning against him with her back to Davis was Mary Prettyman. On the other side of the table sat a man with a noticeable receding hairline. He was dressed in a dark suit and had reading glasses propped on his forehead.

Davis turned away and looked at Campos, who said, "they were here last night too."

Davis' jaw was set as he watched Dumont take Mary Prettyman's left arm and caress it. Then the man sitting opposite of Dumont handed him a gold bracelet and he held up Mary's arm and slipped it gently on her wrist. Even in the darkness the bracelet's color was brilliant.

Dumont took a gold necklace that was lying on the table and reached around her shoulders, and as she leaned forward, he fastened it just below her hairline. The necklace shimmered against her bare skin. Dumont ran his hand along the length of the necklace and then down to just inside Mary Prettyman's white silk blouse, which was buttoned low.

She kissed him on the cheek. Dumont motioned for her to finish her drink and then they got up. Dumont helped her put on her long brown fur coat and then she took him by the arm and they walked out of the restaurant.

Keeping his distance, Davis followed them to the parking lot. He saw the man in the dark suit drive west on Santa Monica Boulevard toward

Beverly Hills. Jake Dumont and Mary Prettyman sat in a late-model Cadillac for a couple minutes, then he started the motor, drove out of the parking lot and turned east toward Hollywood.

Davis followed the Cadillac until it turned into the entrance of the Hollywood Roosevelt Hotel at La Brea Avenue and Hollywood Boulevard.

Davis parked the Porsche at the curb and watched a valet open the passenger door for Mary Prettyman. Dumont walked around the back of the car and took her arm, and the two walked to the entrance were they were greeted by the hotel's doorman.

When Davis couldn't see them anymore he drove up La Brea to Franklin Avenue and parked his car on the street next to the pickup. He climbed the stairs to his flat where he was greeted by Bogey.

He clipped Bogey's leash to his collar and he led the dog down the hill back to the corner of Hollywood and La Brea. Davis stood outside the hotel for a few minutes, gazing up at the old building and its lighted rooms, wondering which one Mary Prettyman and Dumont were in?

Finally, he motioned for Bogey to follow him, and in the cool night they walked back to Davis' flat.

———

There was a loud banging sound in Rhitt Davis' head. He pulled his blankets up over his eyes, trying to block out the clamour in his ears, but the hammering sound just got louder. He slowly awoke from the haze of last night's bottle of Cabernet after his stroll to the Roosevelt.

He opened his eyes as he rolled over to the other side of the queen-size bed, and realized that the hammering sound was coming from the apartment's front door.

Davis threw back the blankets and stood up naked, his head spinning and his mouth dry.

He put on his robe and shuffled his bare feet along the hardwood in the hallway to the darkened living room. The pounding stopped as he undid the chain latch, and as he opened the door and peered out into a light misty fog, there stood Janie Wells, dressed in a long fur coat, Palazzo pants and silk blouse, the same outfit that Mary Prettyman had worn at the restaurant the night before.

Davis tried to shake himself awake and a confused stare came over his face. In her hand she held an auburn-colored wig and he noticed that she still wore the gold and diamond necklace and gold bracelet as well.

"It was you," he said in half-disbelief.

He gestured with his hand for her to come inside, and as she did, Davis closed the door but left the latch chain unlocked.

Bogey barked as Wells took off her coat, and she picked him up and rubbed her face against his head.

Bogey licked her cheek. Wells looked at Davis. "Do you think you can take me to Mary's apartment? I don't have a car."

Davis looked at her, then nodded and left the room to get dressed. When he returned he saw that Wells had taken off the necklace and the bracelet.

"Where is she? " Davis asked, as he helped her put on her coat.

"I can't tell you. If I did it would put her and yourself in danger."

"Me?" asked Davis. "Listen, I can find out, so you may as well tell me. I am in this just as deep as you two are. Same with Shorty here."

Wells was silent. Bogey lay on the hardwood and looked at her.

"He is safe here," she said, "with you."

"Yes, that's why I came back here. Now I am more confused than ever. What's with you pretending to be her and all the charade with Dumont?

Wells put her finger on Davis' lips and smiled, and slightly shook her head.

Davis could see the sincerity in her eyes. She stepped toward him and he took her into his arms and held her for a few silent moments.

Then Bogey stood up and watched Davis and Wells leave the apartment.

Chapter 11
ROCKY MOUNTAIN LIES

Rhitt Davis dropped Janie Wells off at the Chennault Street entrance of Mary Prettyman's apartment in Brentwood.

She had recounted that 10 years earlier Mary had infiltrated the Rajneesh Cult in Oregon as an undercover informant for the FBI. Janie was a member of the group but friction and distrust among some of the members led her to become Prettyman's mole.

After the government broke up the cult and arrested its leaders for income tax evasion, Wells kept in touch with Prettyman, who eventually recommended her to the Bureau.

At first she was reluctant to talk about her night's stay with Jake Dumont, but eventually revealed that Dumont, after drinking several glasses of Scotch, fell asleep in the living room with the television set on. Around 4 a.m. he awoke, and was sick to his stomach, spending a good 30 minutes more in the bathroom. Wells stayed in the suite's master bed, still dressed in most of her clothes.

Janie said that Prettyman had met Dumont for a drink at the Gardens of Tasco after falsely alerting him through the wiretap at his ranch that the police suspected him in the beating of Maurice Otto at the Wilshire Club.

After a third encounter at the bar, Dumont, who had been drinking heavily, let slip that he had done some business with a couple with ties to a terrorist group in Germany.

Later, Wells' resemblance to Prettyman paid off when she met Dumont in Prettyman's place. In the dimly lit restaurant he couldn't tell that she wasn't Mary.

Davis guessed that Wells knew where Prettyman was. He pulled the Porsche over to the curb on San Vicente Blvd. and called the information line for Southwest Airlines. He asked the reservations attendant if a Mary Prettyman had taken a flight from Burbank to San Jose two days earlier. The woman, who sounded like she was in her early 20s, told Davis to please hold while she checked.

Davis held the phone to his ear for nearly 10 minutes, and was becoming impatient when the woman came back on the line.

"Sir, I am sorry to keep you waiting. There was a reservation for a Mary Prettyman on Thursday of this week, flying out of Hollywood Burbank Airport, but not to San Jose. The flight she took was nonstop to Denver, Colorado, flight number 260."

Davis was silent for several seconds, then thanked the woman. He swung his car back out into traffic and drove home to Hollywood.

———

Rhitt Davis looked out the Bay window at the panoramic view of the city below the Hollywood Hills. He took a deep breath and saw Bogey who had stretched out on the hardwood floor near his feet.

"Should we go and try to help her? Do you think she needs us?" Davis said as he shifted his weight from one leg to the other.

Bogey looked up at him and barked.

Davis smiled and walked down the hallway to his bedroom. He took a sports travel bag from the floor of his closet and filled it with a change of warm clothes, including underwear, socks and tennis shoes.

He added his shaving kit and zipped up the bag, took his leather jacket off the hanger and dropped his bag at the front door. He took

Bogey's leash off a small key hook and the little dog wagged his tail in excitement. Davis grabbed a bottle of water from the refrigerator and scooped up the keys to his truck from the kitchen counter.

Then he went back to the bedroom and laid on the bed until nightfall.

———

The lights of Las Vegas were getting brighter with every mile as Davis drove north on Highway 15 from Los Angeles. The ride in his Ford F-150 had been uneventful since he left Southern California at 10 p.m. Bogey had silently watched the traffic out the back window, which was mostly big-rig trucks and high-speed sports cars that passed them on the road into Nevada.

Now it was nearly 3 a.m. and Davis was glad that he had slept for almost five hours before leaving. As he drove he periodically checked his cell phone for text messages, but so far there were none.

Because of the wee hours, traffic was light entering the Las Vegas Strip and Davis drove to the far end of the casino-ladened boulevard to the Mandalay Bay Hotel. He pulled into the entrance and had the valet park the truck. Bogey was awake and alert with both front paws up on the passenger window and he barked as Davis led him by the leash into the hotel's lobby and on to the casino's restaurant.

Davis took a seat in a booth and pulled Bogey up next to him on the seat. He ordered a breakfast of bacon and eggs with sourdough toast, orange juice and coffee. As he ate he wondered if it would be best to either get a room and sleep a few hours or get back in the truck and move on toward Denver. He would have stops in St. George, Utah, Cedar City and Grand Junction, Colorado, in his trek across the Rocky Mountains. He could stop at a motel in any of those towns.

He decided to take Bogey for a short walk near the hotel's parking lot, and afterward paid the valet to bring the truck up to the front. He checked the fastest route to Denver on the road app of his cell phone and found that Highway 15 to Highway 70 would take him there in about 10 hours.

Davis tipped the valet as Bogey jumped into the front seat. The valet closed the driver's door and Davis drove away from the Strip's shimmering lights and into the early morning darkness toward the Utah border.

———

The sun had been up for three hours when Davis crossed from Nevada into Utah on Interstate 15.

He had stopped twice to stretch his legs and let Bogey find some high desert shrubbery to pee on. Now the little dog was asleep on the passenger seat as Davis headed in a north-easterly direction toward Colorado. He drove through St. George and Cedar City and stopped outside Bryce Canyon at a fast food restaurant for lunch. He left Bogey in the car and sat next to a window inside the restaurant where he could see his truck.

As a boy, he and his family had taken a trip to Denver, a camping excursion on which he had visited the national parks at Bryce and Zion canyons. He remembered seeing men with shotguns riding on the hoods of cars and trucks shooting at rabbits and other wild animals on the dusty desert landscape. The trip took place in the summer when he was 13 years old. Early August was hot in the Utah high desert. He remembered how the endless miles of sandy terrain nearly hypnotized him into a sleepy trance.

Now he was about to ascend to much higher elevations of the Rocky Mountains in the winter, where it could be bitter cold and snowy.

As the day wore on, he drove through Salina, Green River and Vail Pass and up to the Colorado Plateau, where he entered and exited the Eisenhower Tunnel, descended across the Rockies into

Grand Junction, Golden and, just after the sun had set, Denver. There was some snow that had been shoveled to the side of the road, but for the most part winter had yet to show up outside the Mile High city.

When Davis arrived at the Brown Palace Hotel, which didn't allow pets, he checked the weather forecast on his cell phone and saw that the overnight temperature would dip into the low 20s, much too cold to leave Bogey in the truck, even though he would be warmer in the hotel's underground parking structure.

After getting the key to his room, Davis went to the truck, put the little dog under his jacket and carried him for the ride up the elevator to his room where he put him on the bed.

"Not a sound out of you, Shorty."

Davis noticed that he had a voice message from a phone number that he didn't recognize. He played the message which turned out to be from Janie Wells. She said that she had heard from Mary Prettyman. She was in Boulder. Wells ended the message with a strange comment. She said, "Janie, tell Rhitt that I have ordered him a Chai Tea Latte, nonfat."

Davis was stumped, but he text-messaged Janie Wells back to thank her for the call.

Davis looked at the time on his Rolex and it was too late to drive the 30 miles up Highway 36 to Boulder. He would wait until it was light.

Chapter 12
THE SCENT OF A RESCUE

Rhitt Davis zipped his jacket to his neck and tried to stay warm by standing in the sunlight. The morning temperature had risen in Boulder to 35 degrees. He used a crosswalk to make his way to a Starbucks coffee house across from where he parked the truck. Bogey watched him from the driver's window as he entered the crowded store.

Davis stood in a line of people most of whom had stopped on their way to work or were students trying to wake up for their first class at the nearby university. As he waited he pondered Mary Prettyman's words about buying him a Chai Tea latte. She knew that he drank only black coffee. But this national coffee house chain was known for its lattes, especially Chai Tea and Nonfat.

As he thought back to the meeting with Anna Stoddard and how Mary had stopped for coffee, a poster on the wall caught Davis' eye and he took a quick breath. The sign was an advertisement for a lecture on holistic crystals therapy and color puncture. On the poster was an illustration of the multi-colored pen like the one that Anna Stoddard had recovered that day from the debris inside her ransacked health boutique.

Davis quickly took a pencil and small notebook from his pocket and wrote down the address of the lecture. Then he left the coffee shop and hurried back to the pickup.

Bogey was excited to see him and the little dog jumped in his lap when Davis started the motor.

Davis drove to a gas station and asked the attendant for directions to the address, which turned out to be quite a distance out of town, 10 miles to an unincorporated part of Boulder, called Gun Barrel. The temperature on the station's digital thermometer read 38 degrees.

As Davis headed west on the two-lane highway, he noticed that the truck's heater was having a hard time keeping up with the cold air coming in from under the back window. Bogey lay down on the floor next to the vent where the warm air pushed up from the engine.

The drive to Gun Barrel took about 15 minutes and Davis soon found the address of the building he was searching for.

He saw a group of people entering the front

door so he parked the truck and followed them inside. A few feet past the entrance, a woman stood and welcomed the seminar's participants and she checked off their names on a list that was attached to a clipboard.

Davis noticed that her outfit included almost every color of the rainbow. Her blouse was bright red, her ankle- length slacks were an almost blinding yellow, highlighted by green high-heel shoes and a royal blue scarf that was loosely wrapped around her shoulders. Her light brown hair was cut short to her neck and she wore a white beret tilted to the left.

She looked at Davis. "Welcome. And you are . . .?"

"I'm Rhitt, Rhitt Davis," he said, extending his hand.

The woman took his hand and Davis noticed that she was wearing a ring on the middle finger of her right hand that looked almost exactly like Mary Prettyman's sapphire and diamond cocktail ring.

"Carol Frieder, Mr. Davis. I am the director of our institute's station here in America. I don't mean to create an awkward moment but I don't see your name on the list for today's seminar. Did you sign up?"

Davis smiled. "Actually, I didn't."

He explained seeing the poster and then added. "It seems your organization could use a more updated approach to advertising. I work for a public relations firm that might be able to help you. Do you mind if I sit in on your lecture?"

Frieder hesitated, then smiled and said, "Many blessings, you are welcome to join us."

Davis found a chair in the back of the room. He kept his eyes on Frieder, watching her body language and listening to her presentation, which was sprinkled with clichés. She glided from one side of the room to the other, a rainbow in motion that oozed a soft and relaxed voice that yet had an eerie and otherworldly tone.

After demonstrations of what she called "healing colored crystals" and a color puncture light pen that was nearly identical to the one that Anna Stoddard had shown Davis and Prettyman in her Los Feliz health store, the hour turned into a pitch to buy marketable holistic products, most of which were over-priced and could be found in drug stores for less money, including "love" and "dream" oils, colored pieces of crystallized glass and books and magazine articles on self-realiza-tion and pain therapy.

It was clear to Davis that Frieder wasn't

a healer but more of a con artist for a lucrative business that had fooled many people into believing their ailments could be cured without the diagnosis of Western medicine.

Davis took out his cell phone out and found Frieder on the Internet. He quickly discovered on a search that she was the stepdaughter of "Johannes Frieder, a German citizen naturopath and acupuncturist who had founded the River of Life Institute of holistic medicine in Hamburg in the early 1980s."

Johannes Frieder had opened bureaus of his institute in several countries and his stepdaughter ran the one in the United States.

When Carol Frieder finished her lecture, Davis waited for those who had attended to leave, then approached her as she packed up her products.

"That was a very interesting lecture," Davis said. He took one of his business cards out of his wallet and handed it to Frieder.

"I can organize a public relations campaign that I know will help your business grow."

As Frieder looked at Davis' card her hand began to tremble. He noticed that her face was growing pale.

"Thank you, Mr. Davis. I appreciate your

interest but the institute has a first-rate publicity department that works well both here and
overseas."

She handed the card back to him and he
again stared at the cocktail ring.

Davis politely said goodbye and walked
quickly back to the truck. He opened the door
and started the motor, then backed up all the way
to the end of the street. He watched Frieder come
out of the building, get in her car, a late-model
BMW, and drive away in the opposite direction.

Davis followed her for several miles to a res-
idential section of Boulder. She parked her car
in the driveway of a modest single-story house.
Davis pulled to the curb up the street and watched
Frieder quickly enter the house.

Davis thought about what he should do next
and he decided to wait in the truck. After about
half an hour, Frieder came out of the house, got
in her car and drove directly toward Davis, who
ducked down in the seat until she was well past.

He slowly sat up. In his side mirror, he
watched Frieder's car turn onto the main highway and head south toward Denver.

Davis started the truck and drove down to
the house. As he approached the front, Bogey
started to bark and scratch at the passenger door.

Davis looked at the dog, then got out and went around to the other side and opened the door for him, guessing that he had to answer Nature's call.

Instead, Bogey raced up the driveway to a planter that was filled with rose bushes. Davis ran after him and saw that the little dog had jumped down into a space between the planter and the house. Bogey whimpered and scratched at a small white wooden door attached to the house by two small hinges.

Davis peered down into the hole that was almost four feet deep. He lowered himself down and looked at the small door. He tried to open it but it was locked. He moved Bogey back up on the planter. The little dog watched as Davis kicked in the door. Bogey barked as Davis cleared away the broken pieces of wood.

He lit his cigarette lighter and held the flame into the dark hole. What he saw sent an anxious chill through his bones. It was a body wrapped head to toe in heavy clear plastic. An oxygen mask, attached to a small tank, covered the person's face.

Davis braced his foot against the wall and pulled the plastic bag through the small opening. He could see the head of a woman. He pulled harder, and then lost his balance. Falling backward, Davis landed on his back and the body in the plastic bag fell on top of him. Bogey barked again from the top of the planter.

Davis quickly pushed the bag off, stood up and ripped the plastic open. It was Mary Prettyman naked and unconscious, but breathing. He took the oxygen mask off her face and slapped her on the cheek.

"Wake up." He slapped her again. "Come on, wake up."

She slurred her words. "I'aaammm alllright."

Davis grabbed her around her bare waist and hoisted her up on level ground. Bogey licked her nose as she laid down in the planter. Davis hurried to the truck and found an old blanket tucked under the driver's seat. He ran back and covered Prettyman with the thick wool. As she began to regain her senses she started to shiver.

Davis picked her up and carried her to the truck where he gently positioned her on the seat so that she could lay down. Bogey jumped in and Davis quickly started the engine. He looked at his watch and noticed the crystal was scratched on his Rolex. It was nearly noon.

Mary Prettyman opened her eyes, looked up at Davis and smiled.

"I can' thank you enough," she whispered.

He held up his wrist so that she could see the face of the watch.

"Get my watch fixed and we are even."

She smiled and then drifted back into a light slumber. Davis found the main highway and drove as fast as the law would allow back to Denver.

Chapter 13

REVELATIONS FROM THE MORGUE

The headlights on the road looked like bright pinpoints to Rhitt Davis as he drove through the desert south to Las Vegas. Bogey and Mary Prettyman slept in the front seat of the truck next to him. He was trying to count the hours since his head had last touched a pillow.

They had stopped at a shopping mall outside Denver where he bought food and clothes for her, including a T-shirt, sweatshirt and blue jeans. The drugs that were injected into her at Carol Frieder's house were still making Mary groggy and her answers to his questions about why she had gone to see Frieder were vague, to the point where he wasn't sure if she was intentionally being evasive or the whole incident had affected her memory. She seemed to take the theft of her cocktail ring with indifference.

He debated taking a plane from Las Vegas to L.A. to get home sooner, but realized that not only did Frieder take her ring but also her wallet and identification, so the plane trip was out.

Highway 15 back to Los Angeles was clear as far as the horizon, it being a Wednesday night had made it an easy drive. The heavy volume of cars from the desert to the city wouldn't start to increase for another 24 hours.

Davis stopped in Barstow for gas and a Coca Cola, and he gave Bogey a pee break behind the station.

When they finally got to Brentwood, Mary was alert enough answer a couple of Davis' questions. She had gone to Denver on a tip that a possible plot was being planned in Boulder by Carol Frieder, and others, to create some mayhem at one of the Hollywood awards shows. She spotted Frieder, whom she recognized from an older FBI sketch, at the Starbucks and followed her to the house. She remembered Frieder answering the door, and then she felt a powerful blow either from someone's hand or from a blunt instrument striking the back of her neck, and falling forward into the entrance of the house.

Everything else from there on was a blank.

She was alert enough to let her and Bogey into her apartment, and closed the door after assuring Davis that both she and the dog would be all right.

Davis stood at her front door for a few seconds, and wondered if he should let himself back in or go home? Fatigue helped him decide to drive back to his apartment in Hollywood, but after he let himself into the duplex and laid down on the bed, his mind began to race, over the events of the last three days. He got up, put his slippers on and went into the kitchen where he found his car keys and cell phone. Davis scanned his directory and found the phone number for Don Ferris, an old sports colleague who now worked at the *Denver Post*. He tapped the "call" button and waited as Ferris' phone rang. After five rings, the phone's voice recording answered.

"This is Don Ferris of the *Denver Post*. Please leave a message and I will return your call."

Davis cleared his voice and speaking clearly, said, "Hey Don, this is Rhitt Davis. Please give me a call when you can. I need a favor."

Suddenly, Ferris came on the line. "Mr. Fancy Pants PR Man in Los Angeles Land, what can I do for you?"

Davis forced a chuckle and said, "What, are you screening your calls from your old bookies? I need any poop from your paper's police reporter on a woman named Carol Frieder, F-R-I-E-D-E-R.

She lives in Boulder, passes herself off as a holistic therapist but I think she's anything but. Check her background, see if she has a police record or has been in any trouble."

He heard Don Ferris laugh. "Your rep is spread well past Hollywood."

"The info is for a friend of mine," Davis replied.

Ferris laughed again, and said, "OK, if you say so. How do you spell her first name?"

Davis spelled it out and then hung up.

He put his head back down on the pillow and fell into a deep sleep.

———

When Davis awoke he was groggy, not sure of what time it was or where he was. It took him a few seconds to clear his head. He looked at his watch. He had been asleep for nearly 10 hours. It was early afternoon and as he walked out of the bedroom and into the living room of the darkened flat he heard the steady sound of raindrops splashing on the patio table.

He looked at his cell phone and saw that Don Ferris had called twice. There was also a message from the agency. He could see Stoddard pacing the floor of his office, fuming because Davis had been out of his reach for over a week. There was also a call but no message left from a number that he recognized as Patty Baker's landline from her old apartment. He wondered if she was back in Los Angeles?

Davis decided to get cleaned up. He took a shower and shaved. He needed a drink so he called the Wilshire Club to make sure the bar was still open. Then he punched in Don Ferris' number and waited as Ferris' phone rang.

The phone rang five times. Davis was about to hang up when his old friend answered.

"Hey, Slick, thanks for calling back. I couldn't get much on your Carol Frieder. She is clean with the Boulder and Denver cops but I did find her mentioned in an old FBI report on a religious group that had a church or a parish in central Oregon, about some time ago. Also there's an old photo of the group."

Davis paused before he spoke. He wanted more than just a photo but he decided to take whatever Ferris had.

"Don, send me the picture and a link to the report. I really appreciate your help, Pal."

Davis switched off his phone and went to his computer which was on the kitchen table. He opened his email and waited a few minutes until a message with an attachment arrived from

Ferris. He clicked on the attachment and an aged photo from a small paper in Oregon appeared on his screen. He counted the number of people in the picture, five men and four women. From left to right, he studied their faces. He recognized Carol Frieder right away, she was obviously much younger but the short brunette wearing a long pullover orange-tinged robe, as were the others, was definitely her. He looked at the others and when he got to the far end, he froze. A jolt went right to his spine. The two women at the end of the line had straps with semi-automatic weapons draped over their shoulders. He wasn't sure if the first woman was Janie Wells, but there was no doubt that the last person in the photo was Mary Prettyman.

Chapter 14

THE INTERVIEW THAT WASN'T

Rhitt Davis stared at the photo on his computer screen for at least a minute. Then he logged off of the Internet and slowly closed the screen. He needed to go somewhere and think things through. And he still needed that drink.

Davis put on a pair of crisply pressed gray slacks, a long-sleeved white shirt with a button-down collar, freshly polished black loafers and a black cashmere v-neck sweater. He looked at his watch and figured Frank Bolger, the bartender at the Wilshire Club, would still be at work.

Davis drove the Ford F-150 truck down Highland Avenue until he got to Beverly Drive where he turned left. As the oncoming headlights passed him, his windshield became a picture screen that featured Mary Prettyman dressed in the robes of a religious cult holding an automatic weapon. He tried to shake the image of her from his mind and he quickly did when he started drifting into oncoming traffic.

Davis swung the truck onto Larchmont Avenue and pulled into the parking lot of the Wilshire Club. The gate was open and he parked near the main entrance.

He quickly walked into the club and saw that the lights were still on in the bar and heard Frank Bolger's booming tenor voice. The bar's regular members had nicknamed Bolger "F-Sharp" and, as Davis entered, Bolger's face broke into a wide grin and he bellowed, "Mr. Davis, long time no see. How the H are you?"

Davis sat down on a mahogany bar stool, and Bolger began to hum "Happy Days Are Here Again." The song broke Davis' dark mood and it forced him to crack a faint smile.

"OK, I guess, Frank. When you get a chance I'll have a gin and tonic, Bombay, no ice."

"You got it, Mr. Davis. Anything from the kitchen?"

Davis said he wasn't hungry. As he watched Bolger fix his drink, two men dressed in business clothes walked in. Both Davis and Bolger looked at them. They weren't club members. They stood at the entrance for nearly half a minute, then walked toward the bar.

"Can I help you, gentlemen?" Bolger asked.

One of the men said, "Yes, we are looking for some information on one of your members who frequents this bar. His name is Rhitt Davis."

The man opened his wallet and showed Bolger his police detective badge. Bolger looked at Davis and raised his eyebrows. "Talk about timing, Rhitt."

Davis stood up and faced the two men. "I am Rhitt Davis."

The first detective said, "I am Detective Cromwell, this is Detective Pomeroy, Los Angeles Police department, do you own that truck parked outside?"

Davis told Cromwell that he did and asked if there was any problem.

"One of our officers on patrol spotted your car on Beverly and noted your vehicle's description and license plate. There was a query from the Boulder, Colorado police department about an incident involving your truck a few days ago in Boulder. Apparently a neighbor reported some kind of break-in at a house across the street. A man of your description, a woman who appeared to be unconscious, and a dog, were at the house. Were you in Boulder recently Mr. Davis?"

Davis looked at Bolger and put his drink down on the bar.

"Yes, I was there."

Cromwell took a pen and a notebook from his pocket and jotted down what Davis had said.

"Do you know where the woman and the dog are now?"

Davis gave the detectives Mary Prettyman's address.

Cromwell made a note of the information, then said. "I think it would be good for you to come over to the Wilshire Division station with us so that we can get a statement, and also talk to this Ms. Prettyman, as you have said she is the woman in question."

Davis hitched up his pants, said goodbye to Bolger and followed Cromwell out of the bar and down the hallway with the Oak-covered walls. Pomeroy walked behind Davis.

"Am I under arrest?" asked Davis. "Because if I am I would like to call my attorney."

Cromwell stopped and turned to him. "No, you are not under arrest, at this time. I just think it is better to give your statement and answer some questions at the station than in the bar."

The detectives escorted Davis to their car, an older model Crown Victoria Ford, and Pomeroy rode in the backseat with him while Cromwell drove the two miles to LAPD's Wilshire Division station.

Once inside the police station, Davis gave his statement while the police called Mary Prettyman's phone number. There was no answer.

Davis told them that he knew the number of her unlisted landline in the apartment and Cromwell tried it. He let the phone ring seven times and was about to hang up when someone answered it.

"Hello, is Mary Prettyman there?"

As Davis signed the statement that he had given, he tried to eavesdrop on the conversation, but Cromwell walked into a nearby office and closed the door.

Pomeroy looked at Davis and asked him if he wanted a drink of water. The detective filled a Styrofoam cup from the water cooler and handed it Davis.

"Sorry, sir, no gin."

For a few minutes, Davis sat in silence. He watched other cops go about their police business. One officer was interviewing a man whose son had been arrested and charged with drunk driving. Another was searching through the purse of a woman who had been accused of shoplifting. She sat in a chair wearing handcuffs.

Davis leaned back in his chair and closed his eyes. He recounted the entire trip to and from Colorado.

Suddenly, Cromwell opened the door to the office and stepped out toward him.

"All right, Mr. Davis, you are free to go."

Before Davis could say anything, the cop closed the door. Pomeroy escorted Davis to the lobby and then wished him good luck.

Davis stood on the sidewalk in front of the Wilshire Division station, not sure what he should do next. He could walk back to the Wilshire Club to get the truck but that would be a long hike in the dark. He took his cell phone from his back pocket and found Patty Baker's number.

After less than one ring she answered.

"Rhitt?"

Chapter 15
THE PUSH OFF

It took Patty Baker a little over half an hour to find the police station and drive Davis back to his truck. On the way to the Wilshire Club, she pleaded with him to follow her to her apartment on Rowena Avenue below Los Feliz Boulevard and help her unload some boxes from a car that Jake Dumont had asked her to hide in her garage. She said that whatever was in the boxes had begun to smell so awful that her apartment neighbors had started to ask her about the foul odor.

Davis was worried that the main gate of the club would be locked for the night because it was after 12:30 and the bar would be closed. But the gate was still open and he was able to exit the parking lot and follow Baker up Western Avenue to Los Feliz Boulevard, and then east past Hillhurst Avenue, until they got to Griffith Park Boulevard, which swung southeast to Rowena.

Davis parked his truck on the street and walked up the driveway where Baker was waiting for him in front of a one-car garage that was part of a larger parking area. She was holding a pair of heavy rubber gloves.

"Jake said I should put these on if I was going to touch the boxes."

"Where is he?," Davis asked.

"I wish I knew," Baker replied, her voice trembling. "He's disappeared."

"Maybe dead," Davis said.

Davis smelled what he thought at first was sulfur, but realized quickly that it was something much more sinister. Baker unlocked the garage and opened the trunk of the large gray Mercedes.

The fumes were so strong that she gagged and quickly stepped back into fresher air.

Davis flicked on the switch for the garage's overhead light. He grabbed a nearby tire iron and forced open one of the five boxes. Inside were several bottles of the foul-smelling liquid that had leaked all over the floor of the trunk.

Davis held his breath while he put on the thick rubber gloves, the kind that a plumber might use to snake out a sewer line. He inspected the leaking container, ran his glove-covered fingers over the other bottles, then quickly closed the trunk.

Davis tried to remain calm but he was scared.

"We've got to get this car far away from here, now. Get in."

He took the keys from her, started the engine and backed the big Mercedes out onto the driveway. Patty Baker opened the front passenger door, jumped in and Davis quickly drove up to Los Feliz Boulevard and down to an entrance to the Golden State Freeway.

———

For nearly 10 minutes, they said nothing to each other. Baker had opened her window halfway down to let the freeway air into the car. The interior reeked from the stench of the liquid in the trunk. Davis looked at her as she leaned back in the seat, and rested her head on the padded door.

"Jake said that the stuff in the back was very dangerous and that some people were going to pay him a lot of money to keep it on hold for them."

Davis was silent for a couple seconds then asked, "Who was going to pay Jake, and where is he?"

"Jake is probably out of the country by now," said Baker. She didn't respond to his first question. Instead she let the wind blow her hair back as she closed her eyes.

"When you were at Dumont's house on Beechwood Canyon, did you ever hear the name

Johannes Frieder or Carol Frieder? He is a well-known name in the holistic medicine world. Late 50s in age, tall with a receding hairline?"

Baker sat up in her seat and looked at Davis.

"I have never heard of Carol Frieder but I think a guy named Johannes came to the house to see Jake, maybe two or three times. Also a man named Maurice Otto."

Davis shot her a look then swung his attention back to the highway.

"Maurice Otto?"

"Yes, their conversation was always about the Hollywood awards shows, especially the Golden Globes."

Davis reached into his pocket and handed his cell phone to Baker.

"Go online and see if you can find any stories connecting Johannes Frieder with the FBI."

She took the phone from him, then asked, "Where are we going?"

"Portuguese Bend."

———

As Davis drove south on the Harbor Freeway toward San Pedro, Patty Baker found a story from a small Idaho newspaper that reported several members of a religious cult that were being investigated by the FBI. Johannes Frieder's name appeared in the story because it said he had hired several of the cult's members to work for him at his color puncture facility in Boulder. Also at another facility in Hamburg, Germany.

Davis guessed that the story was related to the one Don Ferris had found on Carol Frieder.

Baker read the story out loud to Davis, then suddenly stopped. She kept reading to herself and then put down the phone.

"The story says that the FBI suspected that this cult was plotting to make the people in an Oregon town sick by putting tainted salad dressing in local restaurants. Apparently some restaurants were forced to close until the health department could give them the all-clear to open. The whole thing was a pushback by the cult because the town's city council had voted for the group to start paying it's fair share of local taxes."

Patty Baker noted that the story was 10 years old.

Davis whistled. "This is starting to make sense. Your pal Jake needs money, Maurice Otto is still mad because Hollywood ditched him years ago. The Frieders run a phony holistic medicine business that is a front for a stranded religious cult that once tried to commit a terrorist act on innocent restaurant patrons. And they all are eying the Golden Globe awards."

Patty Baker looked at him. "What are we going to do?"

Davis got off the freeway at Gaffey Street in San Pedro. He followed Gaffey until it ended at Paseo Del Mar Drive. He parked the car on the lookout spot at Point Fermin and walked to the edge of the bluff. Below he could see the sparkling panoramic view of the Los Angeles Harbor and the Ports 'O Call shore. The jetty that separated the outer channel from the calmer waters of the inner harbor was lit by the lamps of Angels Gate. Baker joined him to look at the view.

"When I was a kid, my cousin, his name was David Millerberg, used to hang out at a hamburger place with his friends in the Valley. On Friday nights they would cruise Van Nuys Boulevard. One night David and another kid stole a Corvette out of the parking lot of a diner and drove it down to the beach where they pushed it off a cliff."

Baker looked at him, then looked back at the view. Then she looked down at the waves below which were distantly crashing on the rocks near the cliff.

"Let me get my purse and you can release the parking break."

Davis put the car in neutral and looked back at Baker who had both hands on the back of the heavy vehicle. With a strong lunge, he got the wheels rolling toward the edge. He quickly jumped back beside Baker and together they finished the job. When the Mercedes hit the craggy rocks on the beach below, the gas tank exploded in a ball of fire. Davis was pleased as he watched the trunk portion of the car burn.

He put his hands in his pockets and looked at Baker. "For some morbid, inner thrill I have always wanted to do that."

They watched the oil from the tainted dressing burn on the water, then they walked away from the edge of the cliff, Davis pointed to a cafe that was about 400 yards away on Paseo Del Mar.

"I'll call a friend of mine to come and get us. Let's get a nightcap while we wait."

As they headed toward Walker's, Point Fermin's famous old biker bar, Davis keyed the phone number of Mary Prettyman.

Chapter 16
ANGELS GATE

Although it was just after 1 a.m., the bar at Walker's was still crowded. Fortunately for Rhitt Davis and Patty Baker, a couple was leaving just as they entered the main room and one of the waiters motioned to Davis to come and take the open seats. Mary Prettyman did not answer his call but he hoped she would listen to the voice message he had left her.

Davis ordered a Grand Marnier on the rocks for Baker and a beer for himself. Walker's was well-known for being a hangout for motorcyclists and biker clubs, with a few surfers sprinkled in.

But tonight it was a mix of late-to-get-home workers, tourists and neighborhood residents. After about 10 minutes, Davis excused himself and went to the men's room. When he returned Baker was not sitting at the table. She had moved over to the bar in the corner which was dimly lit. Davis looked at her and smiled.

"Well, this is a little more romantic," he said

as he sat down next to her.

She put her head on Davis' shoulder and whispered in his ear.

"That tall man at the other end of the bar with the gray jacket, he looks a lot like the guy who came to Jake's house. He was also in the picture of the story I was reading to you about that religious cult."

Without trying to stare, Davis took a sip of his beer and held the glass up and looked down the bar at Johannes Frieder. He was talking to one of the bartenders, an older man with graying blond hair who looked like he had spent most of his life at the beach. Frieder appeared to be with two other people, a man who stood behind him just over his left shoulder, and a woman who Davis recognized as Carol Frieder. Davis guessed that the Mercedes must have had a planted tracer bug and that he and Baker were followed.

He looked at his watch and saw that the bar would close in a short 20 minutes. If Mary Prettyman got his message, she was at least 30 minutes away.

Davis leaned into Baker's neck and suggested that they leave as soon as possible, but try to make their exit discreet. She took his phone and called for a taxi cab.

He motioned to a waiter and signaled for the check. Then he looked back at Johannes and saw that he and the man behind him were both staring at him.

Davis texted Mary Prettyman with a message saying he was leaving the bar and that he would try to call her later. He added, "thank you, and I hope you bring your colleagues."

Patty Baker slipped out of her seat walked across the cafe to the exit and into the early-morning darkness.

Davis watched Johannes Frieder get up from his barstool and, along with Carol Frieder and their friend, follow Baker out of the bar. Davis quickly threw some cash on the table and hurried after them.

He stepped in front of the cafe's bright neon entrance, but there was no one there, only a cab driver opening the back door of his car for two of the cafe's patrons. Davis ran to the parking lot but it was nearly empty. He reached for his phone, then stopped.

"Damn it," he hissed under his breath.

He realized that he had left it on the bar. He started to walk back toward the restaurant's entrance when he heard a footstep on the asphalt pavement. As he began to turn around, a heavy metal object crashed down on his head, knocking him to the ground, unconscious.

———

Rhitt Davis tried to sit up but the combination of a heavy object laying on top of him and the painful knot that throbbed on the back of his head, all he could do was stare at the ceiling of a moving car.

"There is no use in trying to move, Mr. Davis, you are in no position to fight back."

Davis realized that it was Johannes Frieder who was speaking and that he was sitting in front passenger seat. Frieder then spoke in German to the driver and Davis figured it had to be the man who was with the Frieders at the bar.

Davis heard someone groan and then a shoe pushed against his chin. Patty Baker had been lying on top of him and he watched as she slowly climbed up onto the back seat of the car. She had gash on her forehead that had been bleeding but was starting to crust over.

Frieder turned around and pointed a pistol at her.

"Stay put, my dear. I couldn't count on your friend Dumont to finish the job I hired him to do. He was well paid and then he tried to disappear on me. At least I can get some satisfaction in getting rid of you."

Frieder looked down at Davis. "There are plenty more rotten eggs and poisonous salad dressings to take the place of the shipment you pushed into the sea tonight. Mr. Otto's payback is going to happen."

"The cops will catch up with you. So will the FBI."

He heard Frieder laugh.

"The FBI. The next time they hear of me I will be out of the country. All they'll find, if they can, are you two trying to swim with your hands tied."

He motioned to the driver to turn and Davis could feel the car slow down and then stop.

Frieder got out and opened the back right door.

"Both of you, get out and face the car."

Patty Baker slowly eased herself out and Davis followed. He saw that Frieder's cohort had parked near a mid-size motorboat which was tied to two pylons on a small landing.

"Get on the boat, lie down on the deck and keep your mouths shut," Frieder ordered.

He pushed Davis ahead and Baker followed. Frieder turned toward the other man and said, "Let's get going."

As Davis and Baker laid down on their

stomachs, the boat's motor sparked to life. Frieder untied the moorings and jumped aboard. The man at the helm gave the engine more power and the boat cleared the landing and headed toward the main water way at about five knots.

Frieder sat in a chair and kept his gun pointed at Davis. Patty Baker started to cry.

"Jake never welched out on you. He put you in contact with Otto. He kept his part of the deal," she said, sobbing.

"Shut up," Frieder yelled.

Davis felt the boat pick up speed and he guessed that they were getting nearer the breakwater. About two minutes later the boat passed the twin light posts of Angels Gate and then, at full speed, headed toward the open sea.

Frieder held his gun tight with one hand and the arm of the chair with the other.

The boat's motor was at full throttle for about 15 minutes and Davis felt the strong splashes of the waves against the hull. Gradually, though, the power was eased back. The boat began to bob up and down in the strong current of San Pedro Channel. Frieder stood up with his gun pointed down at Davis and Baker.

"All right, get up and keep your hands where I can see them."

His bulky friend at the wheel turned on a large flashlight and shined it on them. Frieder held a roll of strong tape and bound Davis' hands behind his back, but strapped Patty Baker's hands together at her belt buckle. He ordered them to stand on the edge of the deck facing the ocean.

Davis struggled to free his hands of the taught bindings.

"Forget it Mr. Davis, even if you managed to free yourself, the cold of this channel will give you hypothermia in no time."

Suddenly Davis felt something pinch his rear end through his back pocket. He reached for the spot and felt a metal tool. Immediately he realized it was golf divot repair tool that he had forgotten to put in his golf bag.

He slid his left hand into the pocket and felt for the sharp double-pronged tool. He grabbed hold of it and switched it to his right hand. In the darkness, he scraped it back and forth against the tape until he wore a hole in the fabric. He pulled as hard as he could without letting Frieder see what he was doing. The tape broke.

Suddenly there was a low rumble of a powerful boat approaching at a fast speed. Then a spotlight shined on the water and a few seconds later the small boat was engulfed in it.

"It's the Coast Guard," Patty Baker shouted.

The hulk at the small boat's wheel gunned the engine and the powerful lurch forward knocked Davis and Baker to the floor, and Frieder into the water.

His cries for help began to fade as the boat sped away. Davis got to his feet and staggered toward the man at the wheel. He grabbed the burly six-footer by the collar and threw him down backward. The gun that was in his left hand skidded across the deck. The man got to his feet and grabbed Davis by the neck. He dragged him to the side of the boat. Davis punched him hard, twice to the groin and once to the liver, but his fists felt like they were hitting a rock wall.

Suddenly a gunshot rang out, echoing across the water and Davis felt the man's hands let go. He staggered back and the collapsed down on the deck. Davis looked over at Baker who was pointing the smoking pistol with both hands at the wounded goon. He gently took the gun from her taped hands and unwrapped her wrists. She fell into his arms and began to laugh uncontrollably before she started to cry.

"It's OK, we are going to be all right."

He gave the gun back to her and went up to the wheel of the boat where he eased the throttle back to a slower speed.

The Coast Guard's launch approached and Davis could see its deck lights reflect on the water. A loud, shrill sound came from its wheel house and a voice from inside called out, "Hold your position."

Davis cut the motor and waited until the launch eased its way along side.

He saw two women standing on the deck next to a Coast Guard officer, who had his pistol drawn. Carol Frieder leaned against the wheel house wall with her wrists handcuffed behind her back. Mary Prettyman stood next to a man dressed in a gray suit who Davis recognized. It was Detective Cromwell.

The Wilshire Division cop waited until both boats were next to each other, then he jumped over onto the deck and took the gun from Davis. He looked down at Frieder's henchman and then out to the water where one of the boat's officer's had thrown a life preserver to the wet and shivering Frieder and was helping him climb aboard the launch.

"Lucky for you that you forgot your phone up at that bar. One of the bartenders at that place had it in his pocket when we arrived. Ms. Prettyman called your cell and it rang in his pocket.

Johannes Frieder had been under surveillance for some time because he had met with these guys at least twice in the past. We think this is his boat."

He gestured toward Frieder who was sitting on the deck of the launch, exhausted, and the unconscious man on the floor of the boat.

"We got enough information out of the bartenders tonight to figure out where they were taking you."

The sound of another launch, this one operated by the LAPD, skimmed across the water toward the two boats. Cromwell turned to Davis and Baker.

"You two will have to come with me back to the San Pedro station. I need some answers to a few questions so that I can make out LAPD's report on this. I imagine the FBI will want to get a statement from both of you later."

Cromwell waved to the officer on the deck of the Coast Guard cutter, who put his pistol in the holster on his belt, and then grabbed a thick rope and threw it over to Cromwell. He tied it to the front end of the boat.

Davis and Baker stepped into the LAPD launch and watched the Coast Guard's boat slowly pull away with Frieder's boat in tow. Davis looked at Mary Prettyman who had stepped away from

Carol Frieder. She looked at Davis and put her hand up in a gesture of farewell.

Then the Coast Guard launch picked up speed as it headed back to the lights of San Pedro Harbor.

Chapter 17

A NEW ACCOUNT

Rhitt Davis dabbed a cloth stained with shoe polish into a small tin that was filled with a tanned mix of the wax, and then rubbed it on a very expensive pair of tasseled loafers. He then buffed the right shoe until it gleamed with a shine that was nearly impeccable. Then he did the same to the left shoe.

He was meeting Karl Stoddard and two executives from an upcoming fall tennis tournament in Palm Desert for lunch at the Palms at the Beverly Wilshire Hotel. The restaurant on the first floor of the hotel was still Stoddard's favorite place to do business. The meeting was first scheduled to take place at the Gardens of Tasco but Stoddard switched sites after Davis had requested it. He hadn't been back since the night he saw Janie Wells disguised as Mary Prettyman dining with Jake Dumont.

That evening had nearly evaporated from his memory, mostly because he had made a strong effort to forget it. Prettyman had made it easier, too, by leaving Stoddard's firm for an extended leave of absence. It was his guess that she would not return to Sagebrush.

Davis felt that it was just as well. She had used him, the firm, and Patty Baker, to help the FBI get to Dumont and ultimately stop Johannes and Carol Frieder from carrying out a terrorist crime against a community that Maurice Otto viewed with deadly disdain after he'd wined and dined the voters and still was snubbed come awards time. To everyone's relief, the Golden Globes dinner and ceremony were both presented without a hitch in the program.

Davis looked at his new Rolex and saw that he had a half an hour to get to the restaurant on time. He finished getting dressed, putting on dark brown slacks, and opened-collar blue shirt and a cream-colored linen jacket. His belt matched perfectly with his buffed loafers.

As he was about to open the door to leave, he heard the postman open his mailbox downstairs and went to meet him. The postman turned and smiled.

"Hope you are having a good day, Mr. Davis. I have a package for you too."

The postman handed him his mail and pulled

a small box out of his bag. Davis thanked him, took the mail and the box back into his flat and laid them on the kitchen table. The return address on the box was Mary Prettyman's in Brentwood.

He cut the sides of the box's brown wrapping paper with a kitchen knife and opened the top. A layer of tissue paper was wrapped around a small object. Davis peeled the tissue away and he saw in his hand her beautiful cocktail ring. There was a note attached.

"Thanks for everything. Till we meet again."

Davis smiled and put the ring in his pocket. The woman he really wanted to see again, though, was Patty Baker. An ache in his midsection told him that he missed her. He was toying with the notion that after his lunch with Stoddard and the tennis tournament execs that he would drive over to her apartment and park in the front of her house where she could see his car. Maybe she would come out to the curb and they could talk, or even go for a walk in the neighborhood on what promised to be a lovely winter's afternoon.

The End

ACKNOWLEDGEMENTS

To Elena Howe, a fine editor who made the story read so much better.

To Kathy Varie, a talented artist who produced a beautiful and intriguing cover illustration.

To Siri Weber Feeney, for the cover and interior design of this book.

To Al Franken and Bob Thomas, two of L.A.'s most noted and respected public relations men, and also to thoroughbred jockeys' agent Vince DeGregory, who all inspired the creation of Rhitt Davis.

And, to Georgiana St. John for her valued advice on the female characters' clothes and jewelry.

JS

ABOUT THE AUTHOR

John Scheibe is a third generation newspaper editor and writer. In his veteran career in Los Angeles, he has edited and written stories that involve sports, radio and television, politics, the police department and legal and banking news. *Angels Gate* is his first novel.

ALSO BY JOHN SCHEIBE

Sports Memoir
On the Road With Jim Murray: Baseball and the Summer of '79

Children's Book
The Yo-Yo Tournament